Revenge Tango

Also by Jerry A. Rodriguez

THE DEVIL'S MAMBO

Published by Kensington Publishing Corporation

REVENGE TANGO

Jerry A. Rodriguez

KENSINGTON BOOKS
www.kensingtonbooks.com

KENSINGTON BOOKS are published by

Kensington Publishing Corp.
850 Third Avenue
New York, NY 10022

All Kensington titles, imprints, and distributed lines are available at special quantity discounts for bulk purchases for sales promotion, premiums, fund-raising, educational, or institutional use.

Special book excerpts or customized printings can also be created to fit specific needs. For details, write or phone the office of the Kensington Special Sales Manager: Attn. Special Sales Department. Kensington Publishing Corp., 850 Third Avenue, New York, NY 10022. Phone: 1-800-221-2647.

Kensington and the K logo Reg. U.S. Pat. & TM Off.

ISBN-13: 978-0-7582-1712-7
ISBN-10: 0-7582-1712-9

First Printing: May 2008
10 9 8 7 6 5 4 3 2 1

Printed in the United States of America

For my hermanas Sylvia and Jeannette

"Sometimes it is harder to deprive oneself of a pain than of a pleasure."

—F. Scott Fitzgerald

Chapter

1

The April thunderstorm pissed down so much relentless rain, it seemed like it was time for Noah to launch his ark all over again. Esperanza could barely see through the windshield of his vintage Jaguar. He double-parked in front of his majestic pre-war building and cursed under his breath, angry at himself for forgetting his sparring gear back at his crib. He was meeting Havelock in twenty minutes for a workout and some mano a mano. A little fisticuffs were exactly what Esperanza needed at the moment. Blow off some steam. All the pent-up frustration and worrying over the past few months left him feeling like an untamed, freewheeling stallion confined to a stable.

Esperanza couldn't wait to jet out of town and enjoy the Puerto Rican sun. Steady rain had been soaking the city for days. *Fuckin' depressing.* Esperanza slipped the leather Kangol cap over his head, pulled up the collar of his olive green trench, and climbed out of the sleek sports car. The silver bullet, he liked to call it.

All he could see were armies of bouncing umbrellas as frustrated and impatient New Yorkers maneuvered around each other, getting poked by umbrellas and splashed by speeding cars. The soundtrack was a monotonous drone of a million raindrops. Plop, plop, plop, and plop. Esperanza pushed his way through the crowd, dodging umbrellas, which came dangerously close to stabbing him in the eye. A ruthless gust of wind slammed frigid darts of rain against his face. He lowered his head and was relieved when he finally found cover under the elaborate canopy of his building. Abraham, his longtime doorman, held the door open and grinned. He sported a bright yellow slicker with matching hat and boots.

"Señor Esperanza, how are you?" Abraham asked.

"You look like that guy from the fish-stick commercials, Abraham."

Esperanza was about to step into the massive marble lobby but something made him stop. The blood drained from his face and Abraham stared at him with a puzzled expression.

"You okay, Nick?" Abraham asked.

A weird sensation crawled up Esperanza's spine and his stomach churned. He reeled around, eyes drawn to a figure standing across the street. He squinted. Umbrellas seemed like animated black mushrooms. Among all the black ones, there was a single red umbrella. It didn't move. For a couple of seconds, an opening in the crowd revealed a statuesque woman dressed in a matching red vinyl raincoat and fedora and wearing dark Chanel sunglasses. Looked like a movie star from the sixties. She was staring directly at Esperanza.

Mistress Devona Love.

Those voluptuous lips turned upward in a mocking smile. She appeared almost dreamlike, a completely static figure in bright crimson set against the predominantly black and gray background.

"Señor Esperanza?" Abraham asked, his voice filled with concern.

For a moment, Esperanza's knees buckled and he thought he was going to collapse. He reached out and clutched Abraham's bony shoulder. The sickening feeling passed and Esperanza suddenly found himself galloping into moving traffic.

Car horns blared and tires screeched as Esperanza barely dodged a delivery van.

"Fuckin' asshole, get out the street!"

The red umbrella started moving east. Esperanza was almost there, one lane to go, but had to stop when a "bendy" bus cut him off. He had his arms spread out wide. Another couple of inches and his nose would be scraping the side of the sixty-foot-long blue and white vehicle, which was essentially two buses connected by a giant rubber accordion.

It seemed to take the bus forever to pass, and when it finally did, Esperanza sprinted to the sidewalk, splashing through deep puddles of water as he crashed into the crowd. His eyes darted back and forth and his heart beat faster and harder as he tried to find the red umbrella in the forest of black ones. He surged forward and kept bumping into people as he hunted for Devona. Angry New Yorkers shot dirty looks, but no one dared to say anything to the imposing man in the Kangol and trench, until Esperanza almost knocked a huge, muscle-bound guy off his feet.

"Hey!" the big man in the brown leather aviator jacket and fedora screamed. Looked like Indiana Jones on steroids. Esperanza ignored him.

Where is she? It was Devona. I know it. I'm not crazy.

A massive hand grabbed Esperanza by the lapel of his trench and spun him around with incredible force. Big

Man's gnarly face was a knot of rage and it was obvious he was ready for a fight. Too bad he picked the wrong guy, on the wrong day. In one blindingly smooth motion, Esperanza's hand came up and hooked Big Man's hand at the base of the thumb. It was a standard jiujitsu move called *Kote gaeshi*, which Esperanza learned while still in high school.

Esperanza lurched forward, applied pressure to the bones of the back of his opponent's hand, and twisted the wrist counterclockwise, forcing the man to drop to his knee as he let out a yelp. If he wanted to, he could've easily broken the man's wrist. Instead, Esperanza humiliated his attacker by releasing him and pushing him straight to the wet pavement and into a muddy puddle. Big Man landed on his back with a thud and made quite a splash.

"Motherfucker!" he screamed as he scrambled to his feet. "I'm gonna kick your fuckin' ass."

Assholes just don't learn their lesson the first time. No time for this bullshit.

Esperanza spun around as Big Man charged forward. The bull racing in for the kill. And like a matador, Esperanza flung his coat open, revealing the butt of the nickel-plated 9mm automatic in the sharkskin holster clipped to his hip. Big Man came to a screeching halt.

"Fuck off or die," Esperanza said. Big Man turned and ran like the Flash. A blur.

Though Esperanza continued to search and search, there was no sign of Devona. Crazy bitch was long gone. Esperanza stood on the corner, fists clenched at his sides, eyes sweeping across the crowds and cars of Amsterdam Avenue.

Nothing.

He didn't move. Rain fell harder.

He stood there for a very long time, and as harried pedestrians turned into phantoms, the city became nothing more than a blur.

Joe's Gym was a relatively new health club, but the owners decided to buck the current trends, so they gave the joint the appearance and feel of the old-school boxing joints from the fifties. Sparse. No frills. Harsh lighting. Forget about aerobics and step classes and yoga and fancy weight machines. It was speed bags and heavy bags and medicine balls and free weights. A twenty-foot pro boxing ring was the gym's centerpiece. Esperanza rented the entire place for an hour so he and Havelock could have total privacy. With his second round of fame, the last thing Esperanza wanted to deal with was gawkers, or even worse, autograph seekers.

Stalking each other in the center of the ring like modern-day gladiators, Esperanza and Havelock were ready to do battle. They sported protective headgear, open-finger gloves, and footpads. Havelock, his waist-long dreadlocks tied in a ponytail, wore traditional white karate pants and a black belt, while Esperanza had on black silk sweatpants with yellow stripes running down the sides.

They hadn't sparred in a long time, though it was something they used to do frequently, since back in the day when they were in the Navy SEALs. Their pugilistic styles were vastly different. Havelock was in a slight crouch and constantly moved forward, while Esperanza danced side to side, back and forth, bobbed and weaved with a fluidity and grace that would've made Ali proud. Though Esperanza moved like a boxer, his array of techniques was quite varied. He'd studied aiki–jitsu, kickboxing, wing chun, and tae kwan do. Esperanza mastered a lot of weapons as well, from knives to the long staff and even swords. His hand-to-hand arsenal consisted of a lethal array of locks, twists, throws, and kicks. Streamlined, simple, and very effective. Like every other teen growing up in the seventies, he wanted to be Bruce Lee. Studied all of Bruce's spectacularly simple and effective moves a thousand times, read his book *The Tao of Jeet Kune Do* religiously. Havelock on the other hand, was a traditional shotokan karate man: long and deep stances and linear movements. Hard and aggressive.

Though Havelock was much more sizable than Esperanza's six-foot, two-hundred-and-ten-pound frame, he was incredibly light on his size-fifteen feet. His ebony skin glistened with beads of sweat. Coiled muscles bulged and veins popped. He sprang forward. Jabbed with the left. Esperanza sidestepped and parried. Havelock followed with a wicked right hook. Esperanza ducked, sprang back up, and delivered a fierce uppercut that caught Havelock under the chin and knocked him back.

"Nice one," Havelock said as he immediately recovered and went on the offensive again. "I see my nigga ain't as rusty as they say," he said while throwing a double sidekick, which Esperanza dodged with fluid agility. "You might be able to keep up with me after all."

"Gonna start trash-talkin' already, *papa?*"

As if on cue, Havelock sidestepped, twisted his hip forward, and with his right leg delivered a high-speed roundhouse kick. The instep of his foot slammed against Esperanza's temple. Despite all the thick padding of the foot and headgear, the impact of the kick made Esperanza stumble, lose his bearings for a moment, and even see a couple of stars. Scary part was, Havelock wasn't even using half the power those legs of his were capable of delivering, otherwise Esperanza would've been on the canvas with the proverbial "tweety" birds circling his head. Havelock wasn't the greatest when it came to using his fists, but those devastating kicks of his could easily shatter bone.

Havelock followed up the roundhouse with a spinning left hook kick. Esperanza dropped to the canvas as the heel of Havelock's foot barely missed the top of his head. Esperanza did a counterclockwise leg sweep and his heel slammed Havelock behind the right knee and sent him flying through the air. He landed on his back with such force that the boxing ring shook. He didn't see that one coming.

"Mutha—" Havelock pounded his fist on the canvas.

They both jumped to their feet and continued stalking each other, moving back and forth, throwing jabs and kicks, searching for the next opening. The musky odor of perspiration and leather hung in the air. Esperanza liked it. It was the smell of fighters; the smell of hard men, physically pushing themselves to the limit, transforming their bodies into weapons. Legs would say it was all *mucho macho* homoerotica, but she hadn't spent years training with a Navy SEAL platoon and going out on search-and-destroy missions, knowing that your life depended on the men on each side of you.

"Nice move, son," Havelock said. He wasn't even breathing hard.

Havelock feigned with a left, then delivered a forceful right hook to Esperanza's ribs. Esperanza grunted. *That hurt.* The blow knocked the breath out of him. Made him mad. Really mad. Havelock followed with a left jab, but this time Esperanza parried, charged forward, and smashed Havelock in the temple with his bare elbow, then pounded his knee into his friend's ribs. Esperanza was breaking the rules. If he'd been wearing knee and elbow pads, his mode of attack would've been fine. But he was blinded by rage and no longer saw his friend and sparring partner: he saw a lethal adversary out to decimate him.

Havelock lost his balance and staggered backward as Esperanza threw a relentless combination of swift kicks and punches. He hooked his arm around Havelock's thick neck, twisted his body, flung the man over his hip, and threw him to the canvas. Before Havelock could blink, Esperanza tried to stomp his face. Havelock jerked his head out of the way in the nick of time as Esperanza's heel kissed canvas instead of his face.

"Chill, Nick!"

Esperanza heard nothing. He was on autopilot. His only intention was to neutralize his opponent. He tried to stomp Havelock again, but this time, Havelock rolled out of the way and fired a front kick, and his heel caught Esperanza dead in the solar plexus. The power of the kick knocked Esperanza back three feet, and he bounced off the ropes and fell to his knees, coughing and gagging.

Havelock sat up and ripped off his headgear and angrily flung it at Esperanza. "You done lost your fuckin' mind?"

Crumpling to the canvas, Esperanza got into the fetal position as he struggled to catch his breath. Sour bile filled his throat, and for a moment, he thought he was going to vomit.

Havelock got on his feet and appeared gigantic as he stood over Esperanza, waving his fist at the air, underscoring the seriousness of the situation.

"If you wanna do this for real, then let's take off the gloves. I'll be glad to knock some sense into you."

Though it took him a long moment, and it was quite difficult to breathe, Esperanza managed to sit up and wave his gloved hand.

"Yo, I'm sorry," he said between coughs. "I don't know what got into me."

Havelock stared at his friend for a moment, his chiseled face dripping with sweat and champagne-colored eyes blazing with resentment. He took a deep breath, his expression turning serene, and reached down and jerked Esperanza to his feet.

"We're done for today."

With fluffy white terry-cloth towels wrapped around their waists, Esperanza and Havelock sat on the varnished cedar wood benches, on opposite sides in the octagonal sauna room. Both were covered in sweat. Esperanza's head was in his hands and Havelock massaged his aching ribs. There was some minor swelling right above his left eye where Esperanza's elbow had connected. Esperanza couldn't believe the stunt he'd pulled. He even wondered if Havelock's ribs were fractured. Esperanza intentionally attempted to hurt his amigo and he couldn't find the words to say how sorry he was. Havelock finally broke the lengthy, awkward silence between them.

"What got into you, man? You lost control."

"Seems to be a problem lately." His voice sounded distant. Weak. He didn't like it.

"All these years I've known you, seen you under live fire, you were the coolest cat in the fuckin' world," Havelock said, wiping perspiration from his brow. "The last man I'd ever expect to see lose it."

Esperanza rotated his stiff neck. The intense heat didn't do much to relax his tense muscles. "You're makin' me feel much better, Dr. Phil."

"Speaking of doctors . . ." Havelock's expression remained detached. "You still goin' to therapy?"

Esperanza figured that Havelock didn't find his sarcasm amusing at the very moment. "Yeah," he said. "I think it might be a waste of time, though."

"I beg to differ."

Esperanza winced. "Ouch. Look, I know I ain't been myself lately . . ."

"Yeah."

He was trying to figure out how to make Havelock understand what was going on with him. What had triggered his violent outburst? The answer was all too obvious.

"I saw her this afternoon. Across the street from my building."

Havelock raised his right eyebrow. "Devona."

"I swear, she's shadowing me."

He expected Havelock to tell him that he was crazy, that he was imagining things.

Havelock leaned forward, placed his elbow on his knee, and rested his chin on his fist. An African version of Rodin's *The Thinker*. "Well, then maybe it's time *I* shadowed *you*. Watch *your* back."

Leaning his head against the damp wooden wall, Esperanza reluctantly asked, "You believe me?"

"Nick, I know you been through some shit. But I still trust your instincts as much as I trust mine. I ain't ever seen a better soldier. Ain't nobody I'd rather have beside me in a firefight."

"I appreciate that, *papa*. But you know it's not me I want you to keep your eye on."

"Been watchin' Legs for over a month now." Havelock resumed massaging his ribs. "You still ain't told her?"

"No."

"Bad move, Nick," Havelock said. "If she finds out that me and Justice are watching her twenty-four-seven, she won't be too happy you kept it a secret."

Justice Lightbourne was Havelock's cousin. He was a bounty hunter by trade and a damn good one. Havelock couldn't spend much time trailing Legs because he would be easy for her to spot. So Justice was handling those duties.

"Look, if she believed my Devona 'sightings' were real, she'd be happy to have protection. But since that's not the case, let's keep it on the D.L."

"Fine," Havelock said with a casual shrug. "By the way, what's with that nun she's been rollin' with for the past couple of months?"

"Sister Terez Mychelle?" The Catholic nun was Legs's favorite subject lately. "Since all that bad shit that went down last year, she's been goin' to church more often. Has a renewed sense of faith. Also started donating time to the Saint Augustine's Center for Victims of Domestic Violence. That's where she met Sister Terez. What does she look like?"

"Nothin' to write home about. Kinda homely."

"I went to Catholic school. Nuns creep me out."

Havelock grinned. Perfectly straight white teeth stood out against his onyx skin. "I guess you won't be goin' to church on the regular, too?"

"*Please.* I'm depressed enough."

Chapter

2

Devona lounged in the expansive, Jacuzzi-style bathtub and lavishly soaped her sinewy body with a loofah sponge while she thought about the two young lovelies she'd spent the past few hours ravishing. They'd been quite a bit of fun. A bawdy pair of twenty-one-year-old submissive Goth girls with blue-black hair, who eagerly begged for extreme pain and wild sex, and Devona gave it to them good. It had been a real long time since she indulged in young, succulent female flesh. She'd met them at a downtown S&M swing party. The girls were sound asleep in the bedroom of the expensive midtown Manhattan hotel suite. Devona was sure that when the two Goth princesses woke up in the morning, they'd barely be able to walk.

As Devona continued to soap herself with the peach-scented body wash, she noticed how much muscle she'd packed on since her husband Jason Rybak's death.

Murder.

She stared at the white tulips in the crystal vase at the edge of the tub and melancholy feelings swept over her in massive, brutal waves. She missed her husband with a desperation that often made her fall apart, leaving her with no sense of purpose, no sense of direction. Her life had become aimless without him. Her only reason for being was revenge. She spent a few months traveling. Rio de Janeiro. Amsterdam. Paris. Enjoying all sorts of decadent pleasures as she left a trail of dead bodies behind.

Even killing and torture lost much of its appeal since Jason wasn't at her side.

She detested being back in New York City. But she intended to make her husband's killer pay and pay dearly.

Nicholas Esperanza.

Four months ago, Devona eagerly watched the TV as they announced the "not guilty" verdict at Esperanza's manslaughter trial and she was overwhelmed with feelings of relief. That justifiable homicide defense worked like a charm. But she knew better. Knew what Esperanza was truly capable of. Regardless, she was elated, because if he'd been shipped off to prison, though it would've been easy to have him bumped off, she wouldn't get to enjoy the pleasure of making him suffer personally.

Suffer long and slow.

She watched candlelight dance across the gleaming white tiles of the bathroom walls and started imagining various scenarios, different ways in which she would torture Esperanza and his girlfriend Legs, for days at a time. She closed her eyes and smiled. Her hands slipped between her creamy thighs and the tip of her index finger began to make sensuous circles around her throbbing clit. She shuddered and her hips rose and fell, rose and fell, as she lost herself in visions of pain and misery, and the sounds of Esperanza's bloodcurling screams of anguish, until the whole twisted fantasy brought her to the edge of ecstasy.

* * *

It was a piece of cake to pick the electronic lock of Devona's hotel suite with a special key card. The hit man silently entered, adjusted his leather racing gloves, and drew his Vektor 9mm automatic from the pocket of his rain-soaked trench coat. He reached into his other pocket and produced a sound suppressor, which he screwed onto the barrel of the automatic. His name was Cole Blue. He was an old-school, professional hitter working the East Coast, and this was going to be a real easy two hundred large. Whacking some crazy dominatrix. What a cake-walk. The trendy suite's living room area was decorated with dark, sleek Italian sofas, chrome and mirrored tables. Cole took a moment to admire the spectacular view of a glittering Manhattan skyline. He noticed soft light spilling from underneath the teak bedroom door, which was slightly ajar. He crossed the room without making a sound, gun steady in his slender hand.

He slithered into the bedroom. At the foot of the lavish king-size bed with the mirrored headboard, there were two young women asleep on the polished marble floor. Both were naked and had magnificent bodies. Black and blue bruises and welts decorated their otherwise flawless ivory skin. There were whips and flogs and vibrators and handcuffs and dildos—a whole assortment of naughty toys strewn all over the place. The spicy scent of pussy and sweet perfume floating through the air made Cole smile. He admired his reflection in the headboard mirror as he stood over the Goth goddesses. What an amazing photograph it would be. *Too bad*. With the image etched in his memory, Cole sauntered over to the first babe, who was in the fetal position, and admired her for a moment, then crouched, pressed the gun to the back of her head, and fired a single shot. The second chick was awakened by the noise from the sound suppressor and a warm splatter of blood. Before she could scream, Cole shot her point-blank in the forehead and her wide emerald eyes rolled back and she expired. He turned over the first chick and was disappointed when he realized that neither one of them was his intended target. Must be a couple of her playthings. *Little dyke S&M orgy.* Just thinking about it gave him a hard-on. If he wasn't such a pro, Cole might teach Devona a lesson. *Show her what it's like to deal with a real man.*

Maybe it was time for him to break the rules for once. Add a little erotic entertainment to the mix. How often did he get the chance to clip a beautiful sexpot? Usually it was mob rats and witnesses for the prosecution. Cole had heard all about Devona. She was some kind of urban legend among the criminal element. He'd always wondered whether the "devil in latex," as they called her, actually existed.

Glancing over his shoulder, Cole smirked in anticipation as the sound of running water came from the bathroom.

Devona must be taking a nice, relaxing bubble bath.

He rose and moved over to the bathroom, eager to get the party started, and when he was through ravishing Devona, he'd put her in a permanent sleep.

There were two faint clapping sounds. Shots fired through a silencer. Devona swiftly and quietly climbed out of the bathtub, and now stood with her back against the door, her naked body slippery with water and soap. There was a seven-inch-long, pearl-handled balisong butterfly knife clutched in her hand, which was held up at her shoulder, ready to strike. She always kept a weapon nearby, no matter where she was. The tub's faucet was running full blast.

The doorknob turned and the door opened. Devona's would-be assassin made a big mistake. He should've kicked the door in, stormed in with guns blazing. Instead, he was trying to play super stealthy, and she watched his gun hand slip in first. Devona thrust her shoulder forward, putting the full force of her six-foot, one-hundred-fifty-pound frame behind it, and slammed the door against the intruder's wrist. The gun went off. A bullet ricocheted and the vase exploded and her lovely tulips spilled to the floor.

While the hit man struggled to shove his way into the bathroom, Devona raised her fist over her head and hammered down the knife with all the force she could muster. The blade punched a hole in his wrist and the tip jammed into the wooden door frame, pinning him. He screamed and dropped the gun. She jerked the door open a couple of inches, and as he tried to bum-rush the room once again, she ferociously smashed it back in his face.

Now came the fun part. Devona snatched up the gun, opened the door, and shot the hit man in both his knees. Tough Guy let out a couple of grunts but didn't scream as he collapsed to the floor, the butterfly knife kept his arm up and left him in a sitting position, half crucified. He was blond and wore a trench coat. Appealing blue eyes and a walrus mustache. Kind of reminded her of Robert Redford as the Sundance Kid. Devona hated Redford. She was a Paul Newman kind of girl.

"You fuckin' bitch!"

"That's no way to talk to a lady."

Pivoting her hip, she swung her knee into his face and demolished his nose. The sound of bone shattering gave her goose bumps. Now she was really getting all hot and bothered. For a moment, Devona admired how lovely the pearl handle of her balisong looked protruding from his bleeding wrist, and then jerked the knife out and the hit man slumped to the floor. He gazed at her with fearless eyes as blood poured from his nose and blood gushed from the hole in his wrist and even more blood streamed from the gunshot wounds. A slasher movie fan's dream. Devona stood close; his wrecked face was right near her clean-shaven crotch. She wondered if he could smell her excitement. Nah. Not with all that blood flooding his nostrils.

"You're gonna bleed out soon. Unless I help you stay alive. Who sent you?"

"Fuck you."

"You don't know who you're dealing with. Trust me, they didn't pay you enough."

With a vicious backhand, she cold-cocked him with the butt of the automatic and knocked him unconscious. She'd have to make some tourniquets. Extra work, but she needed him alive for a while, so he'd tell her everything he knew.

Devona entertained herself by keeping Cole bound and naked in the bathtub for nearly an hour. With her razor-sharp knife, a bottle of rubbing alcohol, and some matches, she put Cole through so much intense pain, fucker dropped dead from what appeared to be a heart attack. *Wimpy bastard.* At least he sang before taking his short trip to the hereafter. Cole was hired by a local Brooklyn mobster named Richie Goteri. Goteri seemed to be working as an intermediary for someone else, but Cole didn't know who that person was, otherwise he would've spilled his guts.

Driving her silver Mercedes sedan through the heavy

rainfall, Devona wondered what the fuck was going on. This was the second attempt on her life in the past couple of weeks. Last time, it was two Jamaican Rastafarians firing machine pistols during a drive-by in an underground parking lot. Lucky for her, they couldn't shoot straight. She not only managed to escape the barrage of bullets, she also gunned down one of the Rastas in the process. She thought it was some kind of weird fluke, that the Jamaicans had mistaken her for some other mark. But Mr. Blue proved her wrong. He was obviously much more of a pro, and still wasn't skilled enough to finish the job.

She cruised down the rain-slicked boulevard of Times Square and the electronic building ads created an eerily dreamlike rainbow light show on the wet asphalt. The only other cars on the Broadway were yellow taxicabs.

Could Esperanza be behind this? No. Not his style.

Either he'd do her personally or he'd send somebody much more capable. She turned on the car stereo. Her favorite album of all time. *Two Wheels Good* by Prefab Sprout. Little-known British band from the swinging new-wave eighties. The song was "Desire As." Sweet, melancholy voice floated over brooding keyboards. Sparse. Simple. Complex. And haunting.

I've got six things on my mind; you're no longer one of them . . .

Devona sang the lyrics to the song, her rich voice cracking with emotion. *Jason. I miss you so much.* She wiped a tear from her cheek and regained her focus. Time to deal with the problem at hand. She figured that whoever was trying to whack her had no intention of stopping until the job was done. She knew she'd pissed off a lot of people in the past, but this was something bigger. She needed to find out why. Most of all, who? Too bad she wasn't an investigator. What was she going to do, hire a private detective?

She grinned as a perversely grand idea came to her mind, and then sped uptown to her secret hideaway.

Chapter

3

It was the first sunny day in weeks as the Esperanza brothers enjoyed a game of handball. They were in the park in El Barrio in East Harlem, playing on the same court they'd played as kids.

Mark scored another point.

"Gettin' old, bro. Used to beat me all the time," Mark said. He was wearing gray sweatpants, leather Nikes, and a T-shirt with the Puerto Rican flag on it. With the blue bandanna tied around his head, he looked more like a gang member than a special agent with the FBI's Joint Terrorism Task Force.

"Game ain't over yet," Esperanza said as he delivered a wicked serve. Mark dove but still missed.

"Not bad, Nick."

The park was jam-packed. Kids played handball and basketball, while reggaeton and hip-hop music thundered from portable boom boxes, drowning out the melody of chirping birds. Sexy teenage Puerto Rican girls with wide hips strutted by in tiny tight shorts, glad for the warm weather so they could show off their spectacular wares to the shirtless, sinewy, hooting and hollering horny boys lounging on benches smoking Newports. The air smelled clean. The sun was bright. The day was full of promise. Spring was definitely in the air.

In a black T-shirt and black sweatpants, Esperanza used his forearm to wipe sweat from his eyes as he enjoyed the youthful sexual energy crackling throughout the park. He grinned as he remembered Legs and him sitting on one of those benches, feverishly making out after playing a serious game of handball. This park, which was surrounded by anorexic trees and offered a full view of the traffic from FDR zooming by. This park, where Esperanza smoked his first joint. Drank his first beer. Got in his first fight. A lot of history in this damn park.

Mark served. Esperanza hit the ball. Mark leapt up, slammed it. The black rubber ball bounced off the corner of the wall and went high. Esperanza jumped, swung, but missed by a fraction of an inch.

"Game, baby," Mark said and did a fancy salsa step, finishing off with a spin and a theatrical bow.

Esperanza bent over, catching his breath as sweat dripped down his face.

"Okay, big shot. Lunch's on me."

At the Emilio's Lechonera on 116th and Second Avenue, Esperanza and Mark sat at the battered counter eating white rice and red beans and chunks of greasy fried pork. The scent of garlic and *sofrito* wafted through the air. In the front window, in metal trays and heated by 150-watt light bulbs, was a display of *cuchifritos*. Everything nice and deep-fried. Heart attack city.

The owner, Emilio, who'd been running the joint for nearly forty years, was in his early sixties and still as spry and gregarious as he was when Nicholas and Mark were kids. He brought over a couple of cold bottles of Medalla, a popular Puerto Rican beer.

"It's good to see *los hermanos* Esperanza back in El Barrio. Shows that miracles can still happen." He clapped his calloused hands together and chuckled. There was a paper hat propped on his head and his white shirt was stained with grease and sauce.

"Good to be here," Esperanza said, holding up his beer.

"I've always been very proud of you boys. You done good."

"Gracias, Don Emilio," Mark said.

"*Y tú mama? Esta bien?*"

"Mom's doin' real good," Mark said.

"Wonderful woman." Emilio kissed his fingertips. "A saint. Send her *un fuerte abrazo* from me, okay?"

"Business still good?" Esperanza asked.

"Not as good. I might have to start selling tacos since all the Mexicans been movin' to the area."

"Times change, Don Emilio," Mark said.

"The Mexicans don't bother me. At least they're *hispanos*. Bring their own particular flavor to the neighborhood. It's the *blanquitos* that have been movin' in that make me nervous." Emilio twisted the tips of his handlebar mustache and wagged his head in disappointment. "Lookit what happened to West Harlem. Black people can't afford to live there no more. Fillin' up with white folks with *mucho dinero*. Sad," Emilio said and went off to serve another customer.

"Emilio looks good," Esperanza said.

"Yeah. Nice being in El Barrio. Brings back a lot of memories," Mark said. "What made you decide to come here today?"

They usually played racquetball at a fancy gym on the

Upper West Side. For some reason, Esperanza felt the urge to play old-school handball in the ol' neighborhood.

"I dunno. Feeling nostalgic, I guess."

"So, how's everything going with you?"

Esperanza hadn't told Mark anything about his Devona "sightings." He wasn't sure why. They were close, but for some reason, he felt ill at ease discussing it with his brother.

"I'm hangin' in there. Getting my life back to normal."

"Good, I'm glad. You've been through a lot."

When Esperanza got involved in the search for Legs's niece Alina and conducted his own private investigation, Mark didn't approve, but helped him out nonetheless. Mark was a straight arrow. The idea of anyone, especially his brother, working outside the law didn't sit well with him. He took some heat for assisting Esperanza, but because it became a major investigation for the Feds and led to several arrests and indictments, they let Mark off with only a reprimand.

"When are you and Anita gonna come over for dinner?" Esperanza asked. "It's been a while."

"Let's do something in a couple of weeks." Mark swiveled on his stool and took a long gulp of beer, his gaze never leaving Esperanza. "You sure you okay? You seem a little preoccupied."

"I'm fine, *hermanito*." Esperanza popped a chunk of pork in his mouth and relished the garlicky flavor.

"Oh, by the way, can you do me a favor and take Mom to the cemetery on Sunday? Gabriel has a ball game I have to go to."

"Sure."

"She'll be glad. You haven't gone with her in a while."

"You don't have to rub it in, you know."

Mark tensed up. "It's not that, Nick. I know it makes

you uncomfortable, but for Mom's sake, you should try and go with her a little more often."

"You're right. I promise to do better."

"Look, Nick. This isn't about me, this is about Mom."

"Don't worry. I'm not pissed or anything. I totally agree." Esperanza often felt guilty because he hardly visited his father's grave. But when he went, he found himself filled with anxiety. Maybe it was because it wasn't the way he wanted to remember the old man.

"Good. By the way, your nephews want to know if you're taking them bowling next week."

"Wouldn't miss it for the world."

Chapter

4

Dr. Hazel Yuen's office was located in trendy Soho. It was a cozy space with raw brick walls and enormous picture windows. Rain splattered against the glass and the view outside was gray and grim again. Esperanza was slumped in the soft-as-melted-butter leather love seat, which was the color of mud. He felt like the rambunctious kid who'd been sent to the principal's office for the umpteenth time. On the redwood coffee table in front of him was a crystal vase with bright yellow tulips. It was the only real splash of color in the room, since Hazel seemed to have a preference for earth tones. Even her clothes. The one thing that Hazel wasn't formal about was, even though she was a psychiatrist, she didn't like for her patients to call her Doctor Yuen. It was simply Hazel.

"I'm positive I saw her," Esperanza said, looking up from the tulips. He wore a black crewneck and gray corduroys, which were damp below the knee. At least his hiking boots had kept his feet dry.

"What makes this different from the other times?"

Opposite Esperanza, Hazel stiffly sat in a rust-colored

Eames chair. Such good posture. She wore a brown cashmere pullover and pleated beige pants, which seemed a
size too big for her anorexic figure. There was a white silk
shawl draped around her shoulders, showcasing her lengthy
neck. The only part of her outfit that showed some personality were pointy brown cowboy boots. The leather
was scuffed and cracked from years of use.

"I was sure those times, too. It's you and Legs who
seem to think I'm imagining things."

Esperanza put Hazel's age at around fifty, but she appeared a decade younger. Half Chinese, half white.
Dominant, yet somewhat plain Asian features framed by a
reddish, pageboy haircut. Her most striking feature was
her sapphire eyes, which remained professionally detached as they carefully scrutinized Esperanza's every reaction.

She gently pushed the tortoiseshell designer glasses
up the bridge of her broad nose, and then said, "Nicholas,
as a victim of . . ."

"You gotta stop with that victim of sexual assault shit . . ."
Hazel came highly recommended by an old colleague in
the Special Victims Squad. For a long time, Esperanza dismissed the idea of going to a therapist, but the sleepless
nights and the nightmares finally convinced him that it
was the smart thing to do. Unfortunately, since Hazel often
treated victims of rape and sexual abuse, she always came
back to the subject. "You know that the main reason I
started coming to you is not because I was 'raped'. It was
because in some ways I liked what Devona did to me.
Liked that she took me to dark places. Yeah, it was by
force, but the simple truth is, a part of me enjoyed it." It
was true. It was as if Devona knew Esperanza's most secret, twisted fantasies and made them a reality.

"I know it takes a lot of courage to admit that."

If there was one thing people would say about Esperanza, it was that he was brutally honest about himself and others. Sometimes it was more than people could handle. "I keep having that recurring dream, where I'm fucking Devona from behind, and when she comes, I snap her neck and then keep fucking her corpse. Doesn't that make me as perverse as her?"

"No matter what you say, you were still traumatized by the experience. If Devona hadn't done what she'd done, you wouldn't be as emotionally . . ."

"Unstable?"

"Overwhelmed."

"Nice way of putting it." Esperanza scratched his stubbly neck. He needed a shave. "Regardless of my . . . emotional state, I know Devona *is* stalking me. I know it's something you commonly see in your patients, but I'm an experienced cop. Years of instinct and experience that I trust."

Hazel played with her platinum wedding band. The sound of the rain seemed to grow louder.

"I understand. Men have a different way of dealing with sexual trauma. Loss of control is very difficult. That's why so few come forward. It makes you question your manhood. 'Specially a man like yourself."

Esperanza glanced over at the desk on the other side of the room, a lovely mahogany antique with all sorts of sinewy curves. Must have set the ol' girl back a pretty penny. What bothered Esperanza was that everything in Hazel's office was so damn perfectly neat. Not a pen or paper out of place. Hazel was an obsessively fastidious woman. She dealt with victims of sex crimes, and Esperanza took her for the kind of chick who didn't like sex. Too messy.

"During my career in law enforcement, I've encountered all kinds of killers," he said, voice flat. "Those who do it out of passion, those who do it for profit, even those who do it for pleasure." He clasped his hands together. "Devona? She did it for all those reasons, and more. To her, it's an art. There are few people I'd say are born evil. Devona's at the top of the list. I bumped off her husband. Her soul mate. She's gonna take revenge sooner or later. Believe me. And she's gonna drag it out . . . turn it into a game." He jabbed his index finger, emphasizing every word he was saying. "So what the fuck makes you so sure that the times I've seen her have been *figments* of my imagination?"

The therapist pursed her measly lips. She seemed unsure of how to respond. "I can't be totally certain. Maybe if you tried the medication I prescribed."

Some antianxiety medication called Klonopin he never bothered to take. Maybe he should. But Esperanza preferred his drugs to be recreational.

"Depression and anxiety aren't the problem. *Devona is.*"

"And what will you do if it turns out that she *is* stalking you?"

Giving the doctor an icy gaze, Esperanza confidently leaned forward and rested his hands on his knees. "The first chance I get . . . I'm gonna blow her brains out."

He saw a slight twitch in Hazel's face. She knew he meant it and it was clear that it made her anxious. She picked up the bottle of Evian from the coffee table and took a sip.

"Shouldn't you do the right thing and bring her to justice?"

"*The right thing?* Maybe in another lifetime. Now? All bets are off."

"What if you make a mistake? I mean, look at what happened yesterday with Havelock."

"My mistake was that I didn't waste her the first time. Then she'd be nothing but a distant memory."

She picked up the leather-bound journal from her lap, pulled a fancy Mont Blanc fountain pen from her pocket, and scribbled some notes.

"Do I scare you, Hazel?"

She looked up, scrunched her neatly plucked eyebrows, appearing somewhat perplexed by his question.

"No. Why do you ask?"

Esperanza knew she was lying. Though she was naturally a stiff, he could see her become even more rigid when he said he'd kill Devona. Her tells were subtle, but were tells nonetheless. For some strange reason, Esperanza was enjoying the fact that he was making Hazel uncomfortable.

"No reason. Just curious."

"Should I be afraid of you?"

"Only if you were trying to hurt me, or someone I love."

She closed the notebook, placed it back on her lap, slender hands on top, fingers nervously drumming. "How are things between you and Legs?"

Esperanza thought about Legs for a moment. Thought about the rough waters they'd sailed in the past year. He smiled thoughtfully.

"Fine."

He wondered for a moment if the good doctor was perceptive enough to know that for the first time during the entire session, he actually lied to her. Because in reality, things weren't going so well between him and Legs, and Esperanza was having a difficult time figuring out how to fix the relationship. He knew that sooner or later he'd better come up with an answer, or he might end up losing her altogether.

Chapter
5

Standing on the wraparound balcony of his tenth-floor apartment, an unlit joint dangling from the corner of his mouth, Esperanza listened to the perpetual cadence of raindrops slapping against concrete. One sunny day in a whole damn month. Depressing.

He wore a fleece robe and matching slippers, both dark blue. There was no traffic below. No other sounds. He jutted his hand out, enjoying the cool drops on his palm as he studied the cathedrallike apartment building across the street. Ominous gargoyles were perched on every landing, batlike wings spread wide. Lightning flashed and illuminated the sneering creature. Esperanza remembered that night, after his encounter with Devona; he swore he saw the damn gargoyle move, and it even spoke to him. Made him think he was losing his mind. He waited. It remained still. Made him relieved. Took deep breaths, and then wiped rainwater on his face. The crisp spring air smelled fresh and was invigorating.

Esperanza lit the joint, inhaled the sweet, intoxicating smoke, and thought about his loss of control the other day while sparring with Havelock. The rage. It was a fire within him that he needed to extinguish. It was making him hurt the people he loved. Most of all, he needed to have all his faculties intact. Needed to be ready. He reached into his pocket and produced a couple of sleeping pills. Stared at them. Sleep was something he avoided lately. Because of the nightmares. *No. It's because of the memories of humiliation.* Pleasure. Pain. Violence. Death. Torture. Sex. He flung the pills high in the air and watched them plummet into the darkness.

The weed made him relax. Senses heightened. Mind drifted.

The soft sound of footsteps came from the living room. Legs stepped out onto the balcony but he didn't turn around. She wrapped her arms around his chest and rested her chin on his shoulder. Warm breath on his neck. Warm body pressed against his. Wonderful.

"Hey, lover," she said in her smoky voice. "Like the song says: bed's too big without you."

"Sorry. Couldn't sleep."

"Didn't take your pills?"

"No. And I don't plan to. If I wanna medicate myself," he said and waved the joint around, "I'd rather smoke some weed."

She took the joint from him and puffed on it. Her body became tense. "Want me to leave you alone?"

"No," he said, squeezing her hand. "Stay."

She relaxed again and held him tighter. Her breathing deepened. He could feel her heart beating. Just a touch faster than usual. With her body pressed against his, arms holding him firmly and with such fierce determination, it reminded Esperanza of who he was and what a charmed life he was living. Legs always gave him a sense of purpose. He was a better man because of her.

"Forgive me . . ." It was almost a whisper, but Legs heard him.

"For what?"

"Not being myself lately."

"It's okay, *pa'*. You've been through a lot."

"It's not okay. You deserve better."

"Everything will be fine. Sister Terez said that a man and woman who constantly and openly communicate are like the faithful who always pray to God."

Esperanza raised an eyebrow. "Are you trying to freak me out here? You need a better approach if you wanna get laid. Quoting a nun ain't exactly the way to turn me on."

"What if I have a nun's habit stashed in the closet?" Legs said and pinched and tugged on his nipple.

"Now we're talking." He grinned for a moment and then became serious. "But really, are you sure taking relationship advice from a woman who's sworn to celibacy and a ridiculous set of rules is the way to go? What happened to your ol'-fashioned, bitter, man-hatin' girlfriends?"

"Oh, stop. Sister Terez is really cool. You'd like her a lot."

"I'm sure you'll force me to meet her one day."

"As a matter of fact, she's going to come over soon to teach me how to make some French dishes."

"*Oui*, no shit. If she can get you to cook, she must have some kind of superpowers."

Legs laughed and slapped his ass. "I feel like cookin' right now, baby." She bit her lower lip and leisurely untied the sash of his robe. Her soft hands crisscrossed his chest, tips of her long fingers drawing seductive circles around his nipples as she nuzzled his neck. "And you're gonna be the main dish." She pressed her pelvis against his ass, swayed and undulated. Let out a soft moan.

Esperanza reached back with both hands, grabbed her hips, and drew her against him. She was naked, despite the cold. He clutched her generous butt cheeks and kneaded them as she continued to aggressively dry-hump him. Her hands crawled downward and she wrapped her fingers around his cock and stroked him. The heat, the rhythmic motion, launched tingles of bliss through his body, giving him goose bumps and making him hard in a matter of seconds.

She squeezed his shaft, feeling a hot rush of blood. "That's all for me?"

"Yes . . . yes . . ."

"Turn around." It wasn't a request; it was a demand. Esperanza obeyed.

All she wore was a pair of black leather shoes with three-inch spiked heels, which made her about equal in height to him. Her naked body was only a couple of inches away from his. He gazed into her honey-hued eyes. They narrowed in anticipation. Legs reached out and cupped Esperanza's face in her hands, then stepped forward and kissed him roughly as the tip of his cock pressed against her belly button. Esperanza crushed her body against his, succumbing to the uninhibited fervor of her tongue dancing with his. Legs pulled away, lips glistening with his saliva. Though her face was partially hidden by shadows, Esperanza adored the mischievous expression he saw. Her auburn hair was tied in a loose ponytail. She pulled off the red scrunchy, shook her head, and let her shimmering tresses fall across her smooth shoulders.

Legs squatted and stared up at him, then seized his thighs, nails digging into the muscle. She pulled him into her lush mouth and skillfully sucked, her head bobbing, her fiery eyes never leaving his. The rush was overwhelming. Legs and Esperanza hadn't made love in a while, since he was so damned distracted. He wanted her now. Wanted her with every part of his being. Wanted to lose himself in her passion. Wanted to get down and dirty. He threw his head back. Let out a guttural groan.

"Yes, baby . . . *chupamelo*."

Esperanza grabbed her by the back of her head and thrust his hips back and forth, finding his rhythm: first slow, then a little faster, deeper. As he fucked her welcoming mouth, she moaned, fingernails digging deeper into his skin until it hurt. Hurt so fucking good. Another blinding flash of lightning. Esperanza closed his eyes, listened to the roar of thunder. Blood raged. Breathing quickened. He wanted, no, needed to be inside her. To be consumed by her body, by her love, by her passion.

Esperanza opened his eyes and gazed down at Legs as she feverishly sucked him. Legs enjoyed orally pleasuring him as much as he enjoyed eating her. Some women didn't like giving blowjobs; Legs sure wasn't one of them. She looked beautiful with his erect, gleaming *bicho* sliding in and out of her mouth. He had to stop moving for a moment, because she was about to make him come and he wanted to hold off. He intended to make love to her all night, to drive her to the wildest edges of ecstasy.

Suddenly, their moment of erotic rapture was interrupted. Esperanza's stomach tightened and the air rushed from his lungs. He couldn't believe what he was seeing: the bright red dot of a sniper's laser sight quickly snaked it's way up Legs's shoulder, to her neck, and made it home on her temple.

Without hesitation, Esperanza shoved Legs to the ground and she let out a stunned cry. He dove on top of her, using his body to shield her from the bullet that was about to be fired.

"Nick! What the . . ."

He rolled and jerked Legs through the open sliding doors, into the darkness of the living room, and then pushed her away.

"Stay down!"

Quickly crawling to the edge of the doorway, he peered out, his eyes doing a calculated sweep along the rooftop and windows of the building across the street in an attempt to spot the sniper. Being naked and having no weapon to defend himself with made Esperanza feel extremely vulnerable. A flash of lightning offered a brief moment of illumination, but he saw no movement on the rooftop. Nothing. Esperanza pounded his fist against the polished hardwood floor, and then drew the curtains closed and scrambled to his feet. He looked down at Legs and held his hand out. Though there was only the dim light from the kitchen, he could see she was scared and confused. She took his hand and he hauled her to her feet.

"Nick?"

"Go to the bedroom, close the curtains, get dressed, and stay there till I tell you it's safe to come out," he said almost crushing her hand to the point of making her wince. "And stay away from the windows."

Chapter

6

Homicide Detective First Grade Anibal Santos wore an olive colored, three-quarter-length raincoat. Water dripped from the brim of his battered black fedora as he paced back and forth on the balcony and talked into a squawking police radio.

"You're positive?" he said into the radio, and seemed as disappointed as Esperanza was. "Yeah, thanks. Wrap it up. See you back at the house."

He slipped the radio into his coat pocket and stared at Esperanza with heavy-lidded eyes. "They did a full search of the building. No empty apartments. Nothing on the roof. The stairway doors have working alarms. You need a code to disable them."

Esperanza was dressed in sweatpants and a sleeveless T-shirt. His muscular arms were folded across his chest.

"Someone was up there, Anibal. I know what I saw."

Santos took off his fedora, shook the rain from it. His head was clean shaven. His brown eyes barely blinked.

"I believe you, bro. But there's no evidence to prove anyone was there. Maybe it was Devona, or someone she hired."

"You were never able to dig up anything on her after all this time?"

"Shit, we had her husband's body in the morgue. Sent out photos, prints, and dental records to the FBI, Interpol, you name it. It's like neither one of them ever existed." Santos placed the hat back on his head. "C'mon, you know they've busted people all over the world connected to Bishop's human-trafficking syndicate. But the Black Widow, she might as well be a ghost."

Esperanza's eyes methodically scanned the rooftop behind Santos. "Maybe she is."

Santos reached out and gave his ex-partner a reassuring squeeze of the shoulder.

"I wish there was more that I could do, Nick. If Devona's gunning for you, maybe you should hire a security detail."

"I'm going to Puerto Rico in a few days. I have some people there who do good work."

"Havelock going?"

"No. He has his own business to take care of here."

"How are you holdin' up, *compai*?"

"Been better," Esperanza said.

"You need to talk, you know where to reach me."

"Yeah."

"I'm gonna put an unmarked car outside."

"I appreciate it."

Legs entered, holding a piping hot mug of mint tea. She was barefoot and wearing an oversized sweatshirt with Long Island University stenciled on the front, with a pair of faded, baggy Levi's. She handed Santos the mug.

"*Gracia'*," Santos said, then blew air into the cup and took a sip.

Legs nervously glanced over at Esperanza. "Any luck?"

"No," Esperanza said. "It's like it never happened."

Santos noticed the tension between them and tried to defuse it.

"Doesn't mean it didn't. Professionals know how to cover their tracks."

"Well, thanks for trying," Legs said.

"You know, for you two, anything, anytime, anywhere." Santos took another gulp of tea and placed the cup on the glass coffee table. "Well, I have to get back to the precinct."

Santos gave Esperanza a tight hug and a kiss on the cheek, and then whispered in his ex-partner's ear. "Always trust your first instinct."

Legs volunteered to escort Santos to the front door and as Santos followed her down the long hallway, she wondered if he really believed Esperanza. Probably. They were partners for many years. Depended on each other. Similar ways of thinking. Was she the only one who thought Esperanza was imagining things? Because she didn't want to believe Devona was out there watching them, making Esperanza more obsessed with her?

She unlocked the door, opened it, and turned to Anibal.

"You're gonna come over for dinner soon, I hope?"

"I'd love to. Haven't had a home-cooked meal in way too long. Cop's life. Fast food and crappy coffee."

Though Legs felt kind of stupid, she wanted to ask him what he really thought about what went down earlier in the evening.

"Anibal . . . I . . ."

"*Mira*, Legs, I know all of this is hard on you, but Nick wasn't given a gold shield 'cause he was cute. He's an exceptional detective."

"I know that. I trust him with my life. I'm just worried about his emotional state."

Santos removed his hat, smoothed down the brim, and then put it back on. Checked his watch.

"Stress does shit to you, Legs," he said as he stepped past her and out into the hallway. Santos turned around and gazed at Legs with confident eyes. "As far as this whole Devona thing is concerned, I believe Esperanza a hundred percent, no matter what's going on with him . . . emotionally."

"I didn't mean to imply—"

Santos wagged his head. "I don't wanna get into a whole discussion about this. Give him time. He'll eventually sort out the emotional stuff." He pulled up the collar of his coat. "But I know he ain't imagining the other shit. Trust your man, *nena*. He's the best at what he does."

Witnessing Santos's unwavering faith in his friend filled Legs with guilt for doubting Esperanza. It was all very confusing. She just wanted them to get on with their lives, was tired of this shadow of dread hanging over them. But it seemed like she'd have to deal with it. At least for now. Legs solemnly smiled.

"Thanks, Anibal."

He planted a lighthearted punch on her chin. "Don't worry, kiddo. We'll solve this problem, one way or another."

Esperanza stood behind the glass bar and poured a healthy shot of Glenmorangie single-malt scotch. He stared at his reflection in the mirror top. Eyes were still darkly intense. Still had the forties matinee-idol looks, but he seemed to have aged a bit in the past year. Face seemed harder, more rugged. He was unshaven. Bloodshot eyes. Needed a haircut.

He looked too much like he felt: a man out of control, a man unsure of himself. He was letting himself go and his physical appearance was announcing to everyone that Nicholas Esperanza was losing it. Not the word he wanted on the street, not at this point in time, or any point in time, for that matter. He downed the eighteen-year-old scotch. A smooth as silk, warm sensation spread through his body and his muscles relaxed as if someone was giving him a serious massage. In the morning, he'd go get a haircut, shave, and manicure: the works.

When he looked back up at the mirror, Legs was standing behind him, watching him. He hated that worried expression on her face.

"I'm not crazy, you know," he said, then stepped from behind the bar and faced her.

She took a tentative step forward, said, "I know," stopped a few inches away from him, and in what seemed like slow motion, reached out and traced his scruffy jawline with great tenderness, yet Esperanza remained stoic to her touch.

"I know you're not imagining things," she said, and gave his face a gentle squeeze. "That's not what's bothering me."

"Then what is?"

"The distance between you and me."

He lowered his eyes, suddenly uncomfortable and not even sure why. "You know . . . the trial and all . . ."

She came closer, circling her arms around his waist. His arms hung loosely at his sides. "I understand how much pressure you were under . . . you put your life on the line for something I asked you to do." She sighed as her pleading eyes locked on his. "It's about acceptance."

"What do you mean?"

She swallowed. He could see she was trying to figure out how to appropriately translate her feelings into words. "You were . . . raped. I know that's not the word you wanna hear, but it's a fact. You were a victim of a sexual assault and I can't imagine how difficult that is for you to accept. But maybe when you do, you can finally get on with your life and being you."

He rolled his eyes and wagged his head in frustration.

"You gotta stop seeing me as a *victim*, Legs. I've been straight up about what I experienced and I know it's tough and you probably had every reason to walk away, but you didn't," he said as his sturdy hands rested on and then squeezed her shoulders. "Now you have to accept what went down, like I did."

"Just accept it?"

"Yeah."

"Easy for you to say." She yanked herself away from his grip. "Devona, Devona, fucking Devona." Esperanza noticed something wild in Legs's eyes. There was something going on with her and it was making him nervous. "Sometimes I think you want to be with her 'cause she can fulfill all the twisted sexual fantasies and I can't."

His chest heaved. Why was Legs pushing this issue so hard? It was as if she was trying to antagonize him. "I've been honest about my feelings."

"You think this is what a woman wants to hear?" She poked him in the chest, knowing how much it annoyed him. "How you're obsessed with some crazy *puta*?" She poked him again and again and Esperanza could feel the blood rushing to his cheeks. If Legs was a man, her index finger would be broken by now. "Some super *puta* sex machine?" Then it came: a hard slap across Esperanza's cheek. Hard enough so that he could taste salty blood inside his mouth. He'd never been so stunned in his life. He stood frozen, mouth slightly agape, as if someone had just delivered the worst news possible. Legs slapped him across the face one more time, said, "This whachu like so fucking much?" and went berserk. She punched, kicked, scratched, and bit as Esperanza struggled to keep her at bay without hurting her. "This is what you like, mothafucka?"

Though he fought to stay in control, to keep his emotions in check, Esperanza lost it for a moment and backhanded Legs across the jaw. She bounced off the bar and then stared up at him. Hair covered most of her damp face as she breathed heavily. She blew strands of hair away and the one eye Esperanza could see glared at him.

"Legs . . ."

Legs attacked him again, but this time she was kissing him roughly, pulling his hair, jerking his cock until it was hard. He was going to push her away but let himself get lost in the insanity of the moment.

"Come on, come on," she demanded and chomped on his neck. "Fuck me."

He flipped her around and bent her over the bar, ripped her panties off, and entered her. She wanted it? She was going to get it. Legs's pussy was a little dry at first and it probably hurt, but Esperanza didn't care—he thrust deeper each time and it didn't take long before she was dripping hot; then he was yanking her hair and slapping her round ass while her sharp nails dug into his flesh and drew blood from his thighs as she ordered him to fuck her harder and harder.

Esperanza watched their reflection in the mirror. Faces

twisted. Teeth gritted. Growls coming from deep inside. The sex between them was rapacious. Cruel. Intense.

The image of Legs and him fucking so ferociously, and without emotional boundaries, both terrified him and turned him on like never before . . .

Legs soaked in the large bathtub. The water was steaming hot. She just finished crying. Her body ached. Her pussy ached. What transpired between her and Esperanza was confusing beyond explanation. A streak of darkness painted across their souls. Yet the release, the savagery of the lovemaking was astounding to her. How was this going to change things between them? She didn't know that there had been so much rage buried deep inside, and then to have it transform into something sexual, she wasn't sure if it was a gift or a curse.

What had gotten into her? What had set her off like that? She wanted to hurt him. Wanted to hurt Nicholas bad. Because she was jealous? No. Never. It was almost as if she'd been possessed. *That's a hell of an excuse.* Maybe it was because she needed to feel alive? To feel free of herself?

She jumped when Esperanza entered the bathroom. Her heart beat faster. In some ways she didn't want to look at him, but she did. He was naked. There were fresh scratches and bite marks all over him. Now hers had been added to Devona's old scars.

He handed Legs a glass of wine and climbed in the tub so that he faced her. Took a washcloth, soaked it, and dripped hot water over his head. He sat there with his eyes closed. His hands slithered under the water and tenderly caressed her calves and thighs. Then he opened his eyes.

"I guess we've come to a new juncture in our relationship," he said.

Legs sipped the wine, twirled the glass. "That's one way of putting it."

He slid lower into the water, rested his head back against the tiled wall. His enigmatic eyes never left hers. "About what happened earlier . . ."

She placed the glass on the edge of the tub. "Let's not talk about it right now." She reached under the water, took his hands, and squeezed them tight.

"Sure?"

"Positive, baby." She looked down at the water, which made her body appear deformed. Black-and-blues were already appearing on her thighs.

"Thank you."

She looked up at him and raised an eyebrow. There was a nervous tingle in her stomach. "For what?"

"Sticking by me. No matter what."

The way he said those words, with such conviction, it brought tears to her eyes. "You know, you can thank me for a fine meal, thank me for a great blowjob, but *never, ever* thank me for loving you."

Esperanza sighed. He brought her hand to his chest. "You're my heart."

"And you're mine."

They leaned forward in perfect synch and kissed. But this kiss was slow and deliberate and sensual, and their chests rose and fell with every inhale of air. Fingers painted each other's bodies with the warm softness of tears.

Esperanza pulled away and cupped her face in his hands. "I'm going to have Havelock keep an eye on you from now on."

She shrugged. "Fine." If she was going to have a body-guard, at least she'd have the best. But Legs was more concerned about Esperanza's safety.

"You know, I'll never let anything happen to you." Legs stroked his cheek. "I'd give my life for you first."

She put her index finger to his lips. "I know." Legs lost it and started to cry. Esperanza drew her into his arms, and though she felt safe, she couldn't stop crying as a deep sense of melancholy swept from deep inside the pit of her stomach and her body trembled and heaved and the tears seemed like they'd go on forever.

Legs knew none of this would be happening if she hadn't asked Esperanza to go looking for Alina in the first place. Their lives dramatically changed because he loved Legs and would never say no to her. And he paid a terri-ble, terrible price because of her.

As Esperanza held her tighter, Legs got the feeling that there was going to be an even higher price to pay, and this time it just might have to be paid in blood.

Chapter

7

"I was thinking about the first time we walked through the streets of Manhattan," Ramona said to her dead husband. She spoke in Spanish, her soft voice brimming with affection. "How amazed we were by the tall buildings, the fancy restaurants, and all the sophisticated people. How you told me you were going to make me the happiest girl in the world, and you did."

Her willowy hand swept away the dried leaves dotting her husband's grave and she placed a bouquet of daisies at the base of the headstone. She stared at the inscription: *Fernando Jose Esperanza Santiago. Loving Father and Husband.*

"Your grandchildren are getting so big, and they are so smart. You'd be very proud. Well, *papito*, I have to go. But I'll be back to see you soon."

Ramona made the sign of the cross with the hand clutching the rosary beads and she kissed her fingertips.

Gray and black clouds hung over the horizon, threatening to deliver another downpour. Esperanza rested his hand on his mother's shoulder and gave her a gentle

squeeze as he stared at the headstone. Ramona affectionately patted the top of his hand and he helped her get
back on her feet. Esperanza buttoned the top button of
her gray raincoat while she adjusted the black silk scarf
covering her head.

"*Gracias* for coming with me today."

Seventy-four years old and his mom still had such ro-
bust energy. She hadn't changed much in the past few
years. Was still spry and full of energy. Her dark brown
skin emitted a youthful glow and the lines on her chiseled face simply made her appear more elegant. Her
chestnut hair had only a few streaks of silver.

"I'm sorry, *Mami*."

She gave her son a quizzical look. "For what?"

"Not coming here with you more often."

"Oh, Nicholas. *Está bien*." She patted his chest. "I
know how much you love your father."

"I miss him every day."

"Me, too."

He embraced her. She exhaled and her body trembled
ever so slightly. The wind sang the blues. Esperanza's
mind was suddenly filled with glorious memories of his
mom and pop dancing in their tiny East Harlem living
room, while he, his brother Mark, and sister Gloria hap-
pily watched. His mother and father often expressed their
grand devotion for each other through dance. Though it
was such a joy to watch them get down to a smokin'
mambo or sensuous tango, Esperanza's favorite image
was of his parents dancing cheek to cheek to a Tito
Rodriguez bolero, eyelids aflutter, smiles of pleasure
lighting up their faces as they rhythmically swayed to the
sweeping romantic Latin ballads of the fifties. Ramona
shuddered again, pulling Esperanza from his nostalgic

reverie. He smiled. She stood on her toes and planted a soft kiss on his cheek.

"Feel like walking for a while?" Esperanza asked.

They strolled through the desolate cemetery grounds, Ramona's arm draped around Esperanza's as they chatted. There were elaborate, enormous religious icons made of a variety of stones. Most were well maintained but there were some that were so ancient, they were beginning to crack and crumble.

"How is everything between you and Legs?"

"Could be better. Things have been a bit strained."

Esperanza and his mother's relationship had changed dramatically since his father's passing. It turned more intimate over the years, and they discussed the kind of personal things they never would have dared to talk about in the past. Ramona became much less judgmental in her later years and it allowed Esperanza to be more honest with her.

"I know you've been through a lot of stress. But you two will work it out. As long as you don't hide your feelings or any truths."

Esperanza noticed a beautiful bird with bright blue and yellow feathers perched on an elaborate marble headstone, staring at him with dead black eyes. There was a colossal pink worm tightly clenched in the bird's curved, black beak. The worm was still squirming for dear life. The creepy image made Esperanza turn away.

"This situation is a bit more out of the ordinary."

"Nicholas, you did the right thing. You saved those children." Ramona stroked his arm. "Your father would have been proud."

"I know."

* * *

Pushing the empty plate across the desk, Esperanza leaned back in his high-back leather office chair and burped. He could hear salsa music as the DJ performed his daily sound check. It was a classic Willie Colón and Héctor Lavoe cut from the seventies: "La Murga." Deep, ominous trombones and energetic percussion, underscored by Lavoe's sensuously sultry voice.

Esperanza bobbed his head and his hands slapped the desk, imitating the intricate conga beat. He hadn't been spending as much time at his club Sueño Latino lately. Too busy keeping a low profile, but now that the trial was over, he wanted to get his life back to normal.

Yeah. Back to normal, when you got a psycho dominatrix out to kill you. Let's not forget how it's been slowly poisoning your relationship with Legs.

Esperanza was glad that he spent the afternoon with his mom. Their talk did him good. He felt calmer, more confident in himself. All of his feelings actually made sense. His mom was a much greater help than his therapist could ever be.

There was a knock at the door.

"Come in."

Alina strutted in, carrying a mug of coffee. He smiled, amazed at how mature and stylish she looked. Her curly hair was cut in a short bob. The white silk blouse and knee-length, bright blue skirt and black pumps added a nice touch of class. Esperanza noticed that the waiflike body had been replaced by womanly curves. Alina beamed as she approached Esperanza's glass and chrome desk.

"You eat enough?" She placed the mug of *café con leche* on the desk.

Patting his stomach, Esperanza grinned. "Gonna explode."

She giggled and gazed at him with admiration while playing with a ringlet of chestnut brown hair.

"Thank you, *Tío*." Alina had started calling Esperanza *Tío*—uncle—lately, something she hadn't done since she was six, and it was taking him some getting used to.

"For what?"

"The job at Sueño Latino."

She worked a few hours every afternoon until early evening, doing a variety of odd jobs around the club. Legs believed that Alina would make a great assistant manager. Maybe run the club one day.

"No problem, *chula*. As long as you keep up with your grades."

Her expression turned deeply solemn. She was still going through a lot of emotional changes. Still haunted by all the terrible things Bishop did to her. Esperanza stood up and went to her.

"*¿Qué te pasa?*"

Alina abruptly wrapped her arms around his waist and squeezed him tight while burying her face in his chest. Esperanza hesitated for a moment, and then held her in his arms. He was still amazed at how tiny she was. How fragile. Alina inhaled deeply, stared up at him, and tears welled up in her haunted eyes.

"Thank you for . . . everything."

Esperanza stroked her cheek with the back of his hand. She seemed so much older than she did a year ago. Innocence all but completely gone. A journey through hell will do that to a child.

"You've thanked me enough, Alina. We're *familia*. We're supposed to look out for each other. Always remember that."

Alina smiled and sighed and patted his chest. "I hope that one day, I'm as lucky as *Titi* Legs and I meet a man just like you."

"Trust me, kid. *I'm* the lucky one." The flirtatious sparkle in her eye made Esperanza uneasy. "How you been holdin' up?"

"Still have nightmares . . . sometimes. But I'm doin' pretty good."

For a moment, Esperanza wondered if Devona would try to hurt Alina. No. Alina's kidnapping was purely business. Devona probably didn't even give Alina a thought.

Baby Girl squeezed him so tight and her embrace was so full of desperation it was as if her body was screaming for his protection. Esperanza kissed her on the top of the head. Her breathing grew so soft it was almost as if she wasn't breathing at all. He didn't regret risking it all for Alina. Esperanza was happy she had managed to turn her life around, got a new attitude, and was becoming a hard-working, respectful young woman with a bright future ahead of her.

From the corner of his eye, Esperanza noticed Santos standing in the doorway, fedora clutched against his chest as he curiously observed them. Santos flashed a smile of embarrassment and nodded.

"Hey, Santos," Esperanza said and peeled himself away from Alina.

Surprised, Alina whirled around and when she saw Santos, her cheeks flushed red.

"Hi."

Santos shuffled into the office. "How are ya, kiddo?" He looked tired. Well, Santos always looked tired.

"I'm good," Alina said demurely. "Want a cup of coffee or a drink?"

"*Café.*" Santos licked his dry lips like a junkie getting offered a free dime bag.

"Comin' right up," Alina said, then gave Esperanza's hand a squeeze and left.

Santos removed his rain coat, hung it on the metal coat rack near the closet, and sat in the yellow, Italian leather chair opposite the desk. "I think the girl's got a bit of a crush on you."

"Noticed, huh? I'm her knight in shining armor." Esperanza sat down and gulped down the last of his coffee. "If she only knew."

"Oh, stop." Santos gave a dismissive wave of the hand. "You're a good man, with a good heart."

"And a very dark soul."

Santos shrugged. "Nobody's perfect."

Santos wolfed down the plate of rice and beans and sweet *platanos* and fried onions and steak like he hadn't enjoyed a decent meal in ages. He wiped the grease from his mouth with a paper napkin, put a fist to his mouth, and let out a majestic burp.

"I guess that means you approve?" Esperanza said.

"Shit, yeah. Your cook is fuckin' amazing. If he was a broad, I'd marry 'im."

Twirling a pen in his fingers, Esperanza leaned forward. "I don't mean to be rude, Anibal. But you're not the sorta guy who just 'drops by.' What's up?"

"I wanted to tell you my good news. I finally finished my novel."

"No shit? Really?" Santos had toiled over his historical romance for more than a decade and it was the only time he'd ever uttered the word "finished." Esperanza gave him a high five. "Now you're not jerkin' me around, are you?"

"Of course not."

By the shit-eating grin on his face, Esperanza figured he was telling him the truth. "Well, I still know a couple of editors from the whole Lotto thing. I could hook you up."

Santos shook his head. "I don't know if I'm ready to send my baby out into the cruel world."

Esperanza chuckled. "That's what the word 'finished' means, detective."

"By the way, you're still planning to go to P.R. for a couple of weeks?" Santos said.

"Not sure. Why?"

"Just thought you might want to stay there a little bit longer. Lay low."

The smile vanished from Esperanza's face. "Hide out, you mean?" he said as he tossed the pen on the desk, next to his appointment book, and then swiveled his chair from side to side. He wasn't about to run away. It annoyed him that Santos would even suggest that.

"Collect your thoughts. Face it, Nick. You're on edge." Santos loosened his cheap, red and blue striped rayon tie. "And Devona's gonna use that to her advantage."

"What makes you think she won't find me in P.R.?"

"Change your travel arrangements. Make it a secret. Besides, she probably doesn't know the island well. Or at all, for that matter."

"Thanks for the advice, partner. But I think I'm gonna actually cancel the trip for now."

Santos eyed Esperanza suspiciously. "Why?"

"Maybe I need to get tactical about this Devona situation and set up a trap."

"What kind of trap?"

"I'm not sure."

"How do you catch a shadow?"

"That's what I need to figure out."

Chapter

8

As soon as Esperanza got home, he hung up his coat in the foyer closet and headed straight for the kitchen, his nose following the yummy scent of *café mocha* and fresh baked cookies. *Fresh baked cookies?* Must be a special occasion, since Legs wasn't exactly the Martha Stewart of El Barrio.

Legs was busy in *la cocina*, setting up porcelain coffee cups and an impressive assortment of cookies on a shiny copper tray, which sat on the custom-designed Italian marble counter top. He admired her for a moment, enjoying her enjoying working in the kitchen. She even wore an apron over her crewneck sweater and tight blue jeans. She spun around and beamed. He hadn't seen her smile like that in quite a while. The scarlet apron had "Domestic DIVA" scrolled across the front in elaborate gold letters.

"Hey, *papi chulo*," Legs said, untying the apron and removing it.

"Maybe you should leave the apron on and take off the clothes underneath, instead." He sauntered over and drew her in his arms. "I know you didn't bake those cookies for me."

She kissed him hard on the mouth. "Nope. Guess what? Sister Terez Mychelle came over after we did a women's support group." Legs did a little happy dance. Rolled her shoulders, swayed her hips. "You finally get to meet her."

Though Esperanza fought the urge to roll his eyes, his disdain was still noticeable enough to make Legs frown.

"I wish you would've said something."

She punched him in the chest. "Don't be such a big baby. Just because a couple of nuns whacked you on the knuckles with a ruler when you were a kid, you got this ridiculous phobia."

When he realized how incredibly immature he was being, Esperanza let out a huge laugh and wagged his head. Sister Terez helped Legs get through some extremely difficult times in the last four months and was not only her spiritual advisor, but had become a close friend. He should thank her. If she weren't a nun, he wouldn't be feeling so weird about meeting her.

"Oh, okay. Just let me go freshen up."

"Good, 'cause you smell like scotch."

"I'm sure I'll burn in hell."

Esperanza turned around and Legs slapped him on the ass. "Don't take too long."

With face washed, teeth brushed, and wearing a fresh cotton powder blue pullover shirt, Esperanza was finally ready to meet the nun. He swaggered into the living room. Legs was pouring coffee while Sister Terez admired the spectacular view through the living room's sliding glass doors. The nun wore a traditional pleated, floor-length habit.

"We've been living here for four years," Legs said.

"What a wonderful view," Sister Terez said in a classy French accent.

Legs glanced up, saw Esperanza, smirked, and playfully shook her head. He wondered if he looked that damn uneasy.

"Sister Terez," Legs said. "Meet my boyfriend Nicholas."

Sister Terez turned around. The black veil and white *bandeau* framed her homely face, which was aglow with a welcoming smile. The distracting overbite, a bulbous nose, and skin that looked like it was spackled on didn't help her in the beauty department. Behind her thick, square glasses were stunning brown eyes, though.

She confidently approached him and held out her hand, which Esperanza noticed was dotted with liver spots.

"So nice to finally meet you."

Esperanza shook her hand. Clammy and cold to the touch. Gave him a bit of a chill. Sister Terez reminded him a little of Sister Felicia from Saint Paul's Catholic School. Sister Felicia used to dispense plenty of corporal punishment with her super-sized ruler or her bar of soap for a daily mouth-washing in front of the class. She made sure you never used God's or Jesus' name in vain.

"Pleasure's all mine," Esperanza said.

Over coffee and freshly baked oatmeal and chocolate chip cookies, Esperanza politely chatted with Sister Terez. She enthusiastically talked about how great Legs was and how she was helping so many disenfranchised women and was becoming such a role model as well.

"They don't come any better then her," he said as he reached out and squeezed Legs's hand and she blushed a little. At least his girlfriend could still find him charming every once in a while.

Sister Terez's expression seemed to turn somewhat pensive.

"Why don't you come back to the church, Nicholas?"

He dreaded that she'd end up asking him that question sooner or later. She smiled and flashed coffee stained teeth. It was supposed to put him at ease. Instead Esperanza got this strange feeling in the pit of his stomach. In some weird way, despite the fact that Sister Terez was so goofy looking, there was something about her endearing personality, her confidence and sense of benevolence that actually turned him on. It was freaking him out. Maybe it was the whole nun thing, forbidden fruit? Otherwise, he couldn't explain his odd attraction to her.

"I'm not a religious man, Sister. Sorry."

"Maybe you can discover a new part of yourself . . ."

"I doubt it." The conversation was making him squirm, and Legs seemed to enjoy watching him try to weasel his way out of it.

"Promise me you'll come one Sunday? Just once."

Like hell I will.

"Sure," he said with a forced smile.

Sister Terez affectionately stroked his hand and he felt butterflies in stomach. Weird.

Then she said, "Oh look, we have created enchantment . . ."

Legs noticed that Esperanza's smile vanished and the color seemed to drain from his face. He suddenly detonated out of his chair, grabbed Sister Terez by the throat, picked her up, dragged her across the room, and bodyslammed her against the glass sliding door.

Dropping her coffee cup, Legs yelled, "Nick, are you out of your fucking mind?"

She struggled to pull Esperanza off Sister Terez. He jerked his head around and glared at Legs with crazy eyes.

Strangely enough, though she was being violently choked, Sister Terez didn't appear remotely frightened. She pulled a cell phone from underneath her habit and jammed it against Esperanza's neck. Legs heard a strange buzzing sound and Esperanza was jolted backward. Legs quickly realized that the "cell phone" in Sister Terez's hand was actually a stun gun. Esperanza lost his footing and Sister Terez thrust the cell phone/stun gun into his chest and he went into violent convulsions, then swan dived backward and crashed into the expansive glass and wrought-iron coffee table. The sound of the impact was deafening as shattered glass flew everywhere.

"Sister Terez?" Legs could hardly talk. She was totally confused.

"Call me Devona, darling."

For a long moment, Legs stood there in stunned silence, staring into Devona's malevolent eyes as she came toward her, cell phone held up like a knife. Legs finally realized she'd made a terrible, terrible mistake. Her friend, her spiritual advisor, had been Devona all along. *But how?* She was obviously wearing some kind of extremely sophisticated disguise for Esperanza not to recognize her right away.

Legs glanced at Esperanza, who was down for the count. She was on her own. Without hesitation, she grabbed the bronze elephant statue sitting on the end table and swung it at Devona's head. Devona ducked, and the statue missed her by an inch and flew out of Legs's hand and bounced off the wall.

Next thing Legs knew, she was hit with fifty thousand volts of electricity. Though she desperately wanted to rumble, wanted to take the bitch down, unfortunately her body became paralyzed and she crumpled to the floor. Though she was still conscious, she wasn't able to move.

While her fingers played with the large wooden crucifix hanging from her neck, Devona curiously gave Legs the once-over like she was road kill.

She let out a creepy giggle, then pulled false teeth from her mouth and tossed them to the floor. She grinned, revealing a perfect set of pearly whites, except for her incisors, which were slightly sharpened like a vampire's.

Devona kneeled, but it wasn't to pray. She leaned over, so close Legs could feel and smell her warm breath: coffee and fresh-baked cookies.

"Surprise, Legs," Devona said in perfect English. "I'm sure all of this is freaking you out to no end, but trust me, it's only going to get worse. Much worse." Then she kissed Legs on the lips. Deeply, seductively, her scorching tongue exploring Legs's mouth, and it was so familiar, like she knew exactly how Legs liked to be kissed.

That feral kiss was the last thing Legs remembered before slipping into unconsciousness.

Chapter
9

Pain exploded from his wrists up his arms, even though his hands were numb. Esperanza opened his eyes and realized he was still in the living room. His hands were cuffed behind a kitchen chair. His ankles were tightly bound to the chair legs with two of his own silk ties. Esperanza was relieved because at least he hadn't woken up in a dungeon. Couldn't go through that again.

But what was next? Warm blood snaked down the side of his face from a gash in his temple. There were shards of glass all over the floor.

No sign of Legs.

Or Devona.

She'd stolen the identity of a fucking nun. Esperanza needed to stop thinking of Devona as an off-the-wall psycho. She was a professional criminal. A brilliant sociopath. That made her much more dangerous.

Now he understood all the strange feelings he was experiencing while in Sister Terez's company. Despite the ingenious disguise, the altered voice, the flawless accent, his connection to her was still something powerful and very much alive.

When Sister Terez said, "Oh look, we have created enchantment . . ."

He knew.

It was the same quote Devona had said to him in the
bowels of her private dungeon, right before turning his
world upside down. The line stuck in his mind for weeks.
He'd heard it somewhere before. Finally, he Googled it
and discovered that it was a quote uttered by Blanche
DuBois in *A Streetcar Named Desire*. When Devona said it
earlier, she knew he'd finally recognize her.

It's her way of having a fun time.

The room turned cold and the hairs on the back of his
neck stood up.

"Hello, my slave," Devona said from behind
Esperanza. He clamped his eyes shut for a moment, inhaled deeply. *Stay in control.* He opened his eyes and
Devona stood before him, still wearing the nun's habit.
She expertly flicked a Filipino butterfly knife open and
closed. Light glinted off the shiny blade. He wondered
how many throats she'd slit open with that same knife.
All of Esperanza's childish nightmares of evil nuns had
suddenly become a reality. Why was he finding it so difficult to swallow? Or talk, or move, for that matter?

Devona tugged the tip of her bulbous nose a couple of
times, and finally peeled it off. Latex. She peeled off
other pieces of latex from her face, slowly revealing the
lovely, unblemished skin underneath.

"I have a friend who does special make-up effects for
the movies. Taught me a lot of the tricks of the trade.
Pretty neat, huh?" she said.

She climbed on his lap and straddled him. Esperanza
attempted to speak again but was unable to utter a word.
Saliva dripped down the side of his mouth.

"Don't bother to try to talk. I gave you a shot of pancuronium. It's the same stuff they give you before a lethal injection. You're temporarily paralyzed." She wiped the spittle from his chin with the sleeve of her habit. "I'm gonna keep this real brief. An associate of mine has taken Legs somewhere for safekeeping. Though I know you think she's getting raped and tortured, she's not. Not yet, anyway." Devona lovingly stroked his hair and caressed his face. "See, I need your help. Somebody's trying to kill me. And I need you to find out who. You do this and I won't touch a hair on your pretty little girlfriend's head." Devona squeezed his face tightly. "I promise."

Someone's trying to kill her? What a shock.

Esperanza figured the list of possible suspects would be endless. Or was all of this a part of some elaborate ruse?

"You try and fuck me over?" Devona continued. "Imagine what I'll put Legs through. Oh, that's right, you don't have to imagine it. All you gotta do is *remember*."

His stomach started doing back flips and the room began to spin. She slapped him hard across the face. It stung and brought disturbing memories flashing back. He didn't even want to think about what she'd do to Legs. Just the idea terrified him.

"I'm gonna leave a cell phone on the kitchen table. In a couple of hours, I'll call you with instructions. By then the drug will have worn off and you'll be ready to get to work." Devona leaned close and leisurely licked his face, then whispered in his ear. "I don't have to give you the whole don't go to the cops speech?" She gazed at him and smirked. "Didn't think so."

Devona rose, took a step back, then viciously kicked Esperanza in the chest. The chair tumbled backward and when he hit the floor, the impact of his weight against the heavy wood of the chair back and onto his handcuffed hands felt as if his bones had been broken. Raising her knee, Devona was about to stomp his face, but she froze in midair and then pulled her thick black clog away. "As much as I'd like to hurt you some more, I need you in one piece. Still . . ." Standing directly over his head, Devona pulled the hem of her habit above her waist and Esperanza found himself staring up at her clean-shaven pussy. She was gleaming wet and her sex-scent was intoxicating. She squatted low, gyrated her hips, and said, "Doesn't mean I can't humiliate you."

He expected her to sit on his face and suffocate him.

Instead, Devona pissed on him.

Esperanza squeezed his eyes and mouth tight as a stream of warm urine splashed his face. Despite his mouth being closed, he tasted the sourness of the urine as Devona giggled crazily.

He wanted to kill her.

Wanted to fuck her.

The worst part of it all was, he knew this was only the beginning. Now that Devona had reentered his life, he was about to take another long, torturous boat ride down the River Styx, except Cerberus would be guarding the gates of hell with a pair of 9mms.

And this time, Esperanza might not make it back.

Her body ached and a jackhammer was going off in her head. Where was she? Curled up on a flimsy canvas army cot in some kind of portable aluminum cage. Maybe ten by ten feet. It took a lot of effort but Legs managed to sit up. The cage seemed to be in the middle of an enormous basement of an apartment building. Legs doubled over and clutched her stomach as she fought off a wave of nausea. She was so angry with herself. If she'd paid more attention. If she'd listened to Esperanza. If she'd believed him when he said that Devona was after them, stalking them, hunting them. If she hadn't let her guard down and let herself become so close with Sister Terez . . . Devona. She wouldn't be in this mess.

She was still having an incredibly difficult time accepting the fact that her kind, loving friend was a psychopath out for revenge.

Where am I? How am I going to get the hell out of here? Legs stood up and her knees buckled, since she was still a little woozy from the jolt of electricity. She held on to the bars of the cage to keep steady and took in her dank surroundings. There was a huge boiler, and on the other end, a flight of concrete stairs that ended at a metal door. The walls were cinderblock. Rusty overhead pipes incessantly dripped water. Legs's eyes stopped at a wooden workbench. On top of the bench there were whips, flogs, knives, and other elaborate torture devices. Her heart started to pound against her chest and she thought she might hyperventilate.

"Hello! Let me the fuck outta here!"

Fear was soon replaced by pure hatred. She wanted to face Devona. Wanted to grab her by the neck and strangle her. Kill her with her bare hands.

Legs heard the heavy metal door unlock. It opened and she could see the ominous silhouette of a huge figure standing in the doorway. A man. More like a giant. His heavy boots pounded loudly as he marched down the stairs.

She took a step back.

He faced her. Had to be nearly seven feet tall and three hundred and fifty pounds of bulging muscle. Made Havelock seem small. The giant wore tight black leather pants, combat boots, and a leather S&M mask with a zipper mouth and eyes, and dozens of pointy, gleaming metal spikes. His piercing aqua blue eyes showed no emotion.

"My name is Otto. I'm not going to hurt you." He spoke with a slight Eastern European accent. Polish? Yugoslavian? His massive hand jutted through the bars and he held out a bottle of water.

Legs wanted the water, she was so fucking thirsty. But she hesitated.

"Where the fuck is Devona?"

"Mistress Love will be here soon." He said her name with such reverence, you'd think he was talking about the pope. His voice was a soothing baritone. "Are you hungry?"

"No." She carefully reached out and took the bottle. It was sealed, so it was safe. "Where am I?"

"You know I can't answer that. You're safe. For now. As long as your boyfriend does what our Mistress asked him to do."

Legs was utterly confused. What the hell was the giant in leather talking about?

"And what's that?"

"No more questions. I'll be back later with some food."

He turned and marched back up the stairs, disappeared through the door, and locked it behind him.

Legs opened the bottle of water and chugged it down. She tossed the empty plastic bottle to the floor, then sat back down on the cot and roughly scratched her head.

Was Devona keeping Esperanza captive in some other location? *Is that* puta *hurting him?* She fought back hot tears and wondered if Esperanza would be able to get the both of them out of this jam.

Her blood turned cold. She knew Devona was a monster. She'd broken Esperanza, the tough-as-nails ex-Navy SEAL and ex-cop, put him through unimaginable pain and humiliation, and almost robbed him of his sanity.

Legs tried not to think about it. Tried not to think about what would happen when Devona came for her.

There was a red plastic bucket in the corner of her cage. She rushed over to it, kneeled, and vomited until she practically passed out.

Chapter
10

Devona had left the handcuff keys on the floor next to Esperanza. As soon as he regained the ability to move, and though it was a major struggle, he finally managed to grab the keys and unlock the handcuffs. First thing he did was call Havelock, who showed up twenty minutes later with his cousin Justice tagging along.

"Don't blame yo'self, Esperanza," Justice said. "Havelock asked me to do a background check on the nun. Everything seemed to be on the up-and-up."

The small cell phone sat on the kitchen table and Esperanza stared at it like it was a bomb about to go off. He pulled a soft cashmere v-neck sweater over his damp hair. Though he'd taken a shower, he swore he still reeked of urine. The cut on his temple was bandaged and at least it wouldn't require stitches.

"You know nothin' gets by us," Havelock said. He was sitting opposite Esperanza at the table. Wore a red turtleneck and a well-worn leather Avirex aviator jacket.

"Devona stole the nun's identity," Esperanza said.

"Which means the real Sister Terez is probably doin' the big sleep," Justice said while leaning against the kitchen counter, twirling a silver dollar between his fingers. He was a bit shorter than Esperanza but widely built. High-yellow skin. A black do-rag on his head. Baggy denim jeans hung low. An oversized T-shirt featuring Al Pacino as Tony Montana in *Scarface* brandishing a humongous machine gun and a sneer. Justice looked like any other homeboy you'd see chillin' on any street corner in any Chocolate City, USA. Except he was a pro when it came down to tracking people. Justice was also exceptional at getting any kind of information needed: rap sheets, financial transactions, building blueprints, you name it. Esperanza never bothered to ask how; he simply knew Justice was able to get it done.

"So what's the plan?" Havelock asked.

"Gotta wait for the call first. Then figure out a way to find Legs while I help Devona."

Esperanza tried not to imagine what Legs might be experiencing right at the moment. All he could do was hope that Devona would keep her word and not hurt her.

Justice stroked his cleft chin. His mustache and goatee were so finely trimmed they were practically invisible. He pursed his big, ashy lips, which were in desperate need of some ChapStick.

"Ya think this might all be some kind of setup?"

Esperanza shook his head. "Doubt it. Devona could've snatched Legs at any time. She likes games but this ain't her style. I think she's telling the truth. I'm sure there's a whole lot of motherfuckers who'd like to see her dead."

"Which means it's gonna be a bitch to find out exactly who—"

The cell phone rang. The disco hit "I Will Survive" was the ring tone. Esperanza grabbed it and flipped it open.

"Yeah."

"Hello, Nicholas."

"I wanna talk to Legs."

"Sure."

Legs got on the phone. "Nick?"

"You okay, baby?"

"Yeah." She sounded incredibly calm. *Wait a minute, how do I know it's really her? Devona's a gifted mimic.*

"What's my mother's maiden name?"

"Machicote."

Esperanza sighed with relief. "Has she hurt you?"

"No. I'm fine."

"Do you have any idea where she's holding you?"

In Spanish, she said, "Some kind of basement."

He heard a noise, and then Devona was on the line again and spoke in fluent Spanish with a hint of an Argentine accent.

"Don't play games. Your girl's safe. So let's get down to business."

"Fine. How do we play this?"

"Keep my cell on you at all times. Don't bother to try and track me, I'll be calling from different disposable cell phones. Meet me in an hour at Club Habanero. Twenty-second Street between Tenth and Eleventh. And I'll fill you in. Wear a nice suit. I hope you know how to tango."

"What?" She hung up.

Esperanza closed the cell and slipped it in his pocket.

"What did she say?" Havelock asked.

"Not much. I gotta meet her in an hour."

"Want us to follow?"

Esperanza turned to Justice. "How quickly can you get your hands on a tracking device?"

Chapter

11

Legs was relieved that she got a chance to speak with Esperanza, even if it was only briefly. At least she knew he was okay.

Devona slipped the cell phone in the pocket of her fashionable ankle-length leather coat. All this time Devona had looked like a homely, middle-aged nun. Seeing her now, as her true self, took Legs's breath away. She was a stunning creature who oozed sexuality from every pore. Exotic Eastern European features. Fierce hazel eyes. Shoulder-length strawberry-blond hair with straight-cut bangs. Devona wore a black silk minidress with spaghetti straps, slit high up the front, designer stilettos with gleaming metal heels, sheer silk stockings. Body to kill for. There was nothing ordinary about Devona.

By the way she was dressed, it appeared as if she was going out partying.

Devona brushed away shiny strands of hair from her sublime face and glanced at the uneaten tray of food on the floor.

"No use starving, sweetheart," she said. "You're gonna be here for a while."

"Fuck you."

"Oh, don't be mad. I'm still your BFF."

Best friend forever.

Devona smiled with glee. For four months she had made Legs believe she was a close friend. Legs had revealed so many intimate details about her life, her relationship with Esperanza, her family. Her desires. Her disappointments.

The funny part was Legs often discussed with "Sister Terez" her fascination with Devona. How the dominatrix was constantly in her thoughts, not only because of what she'd done to Esperanza, but the fact that Devona seemed to be some kind of force of nature who could turn even the most powerful of men to mush.

Legs sat on the edge of the cot debating her next move. Devona was a few inches taller and maybe twenty pounds heavier. Except it was all muscle. Legs wondered if she could take down the dominatrix. In high school Legs was involved in her share of wild, *barrio* girl street fights, and over the years Esperanza taught her some basic self-defense moves, but she was uncertain of the extent of Devona's pugilistic skills. She knew Devona was a ruthless killer, so she'd be taking a huge risk if she tried to throw down with her. And even if by some stroke of luck she bested Devona, there'd still be her giant slave to contend with.

"Don't even think of trying anything stupid, Legs," Devona said. "You'd only end up getting hurt. So just be a good girl and behave yourself."

Legs loathed the fact that Devona was able to read her with such facility. But then again, Devona knew her extremely well, and all Legs knew was some fictitious nun. A bunch of lies.

Legs stood up. Her body still ached. "Why are you doing this?"

"Survival."

"Gotta give you credit. You're one hell of a fucking actress."

"To tell you the truth, I actually enjoyed spending time with you. I can see why Esperanza's so madly in love."

"You're not gonna get away with this."

"You know something, Legs? All those intimate conversations we shared about your relationship with Nick? The one thing that always amused me most was how you tried to categorize him as a victim. I know he admitted to plenty of stuff. But he didn't tell you *everything*. Didn't tell you how much he enjoyed fucking me." Legs stuffed her hands into the pockets of her jeans and bit down on her tongue. "It's not like I gave him Viagra or anything. That big, hard cock was all his. Then, when I fucked him? At first, he was enjoying it big time. Begged for more. Wasn't until I got real rough that he cried like a baby. To tell you the truth, I'm looking forward to doing it all over again. Maybe have you watch . . ."

Though she tried to stay in control, Devona's words, her sarcastic tone of voice, the arrogant smirk, made Legs snap. She lunged forward and threw a punch at Devona, who easily blocked the blow with her forearm. The next thing Legs knew, Devona was behind her, put her in a painful arm lock, and shoved her face first between the bars of the cage.

Devona's soft lips brushed against Legs's ear.

"I've killed more men with my bare hands than I can remember. You ever try something like that again?" Devona roughly jerked Legs's arm up and Legs cried out. "I'll break your arm."

"You fuckin' bitch."

Devona thrust her crotch against Legs's ass, and her free hand reached under Legs's shirt and fondled her breasts. When Legs tried to fight it, Devona jerked her arm again, delivering a shot of intense pain.

While gently pinching Legs's nipples, Devona continued to rub up against her, and her breathing became heavier. She kissed the back of Legs's neck as her dry humping intensified.

"I wanna eat you alive. Just like Nicholas, you got a darkness in you. But because you're a woman, you're even more afraid to explore it. I'm sure you've done a few naughty things with Nicholas. What? A threesome? Some light bondage? Maybe some spanking? Still boring vanilla sex." Devona's erotic gyrations decelerated and her rough touching transformed into the most gentle caresses. Legs shut her eyes as tears streamed down her cheeks. She wanted to kill the bitch, yet she was mesmerized by Devona's voice, her warm breath, her intoxicating feminine scent, her confidently seductive touch.

Fight it. Don't let her play you again.

"You gotta tap into your true power as a woman, Legs," Devona continued. "Forget society's rules. Forget morality and all that Catholic guilt you have." She kissed and licked Legs's neck and ear, sending tingles of pleasure through her body. Legs couldn't believe this power Devona had; it was almost as if she was hypnotized by her. She was beginning to understand Esperanza's obsession with Devona. "You and other so-called feminists think that a woman using her sexuality is a weakness. All that intellectual rhetoric about empowerment? Bullshit. Sex is power. Femininity is power. Yes, we're fucking equal to men, but we're not the same. We're the anima. When I talk about sex is power, I'm not talking about some dumb stripper giving twenty-dollar lap dances. I'm talking about making a man bow down to you."

Legs wondered why Devona was telling her all of this. What was she trying to prove to her?

"Take what you want, when you want it," Devona continued, and between words, kissed and licked and rubbed and touched. "How do you think I turned your man out? Why do you think he's so obsessed with me? If you truly gave him what he wanted, I'd only be a distant memory. But you're too busy playing the proper girl. Be your true self."

Legs thought about a few nights ago, when she lost it and she became violent, and she and Esperanza had that rough, feral sex. For the first time she surrendered to something dark inside herself.

Devona abruptly released Legs and stepped back. Legs tightly gripped the bars and opened her eyes. She was furious. Confused. Aroused. She didn't want to turn around and face her tormentor, but finally did.

Those piercing eyes stared back. They were like Esperanza had described. Beautiful. Mesmerizing. Evil. Promising something forbidden.

Devona moistened her lips with the tip of her tongue, then smoothed down her dress.

She threw Legs a kiss and strutted out, locking the cage door behind her. The sound of her clicking heels faded in the distance.

What was this strange power of seduction Devona possessed? Legs had never encountered anyone like her before. Devona's ferocious gaze left her shaken to her very core.

At first, Legs hugged herself. Then she impatiently paced back and forth. Then she let out an insane scream bursting with rage. Finally, she calmed down and kneeled on the concrete floor, closed her eyes, brought her palms together, lowered her head, and prayed. In spite of the fact that the very person who'd helped her regain her faith in the church was the person who now led her into the darkness, Legs's faith was still strong and it was still her own.

"Forgive us our trespasses," she whispered, "as we forgive those who trespass against us."

She prayed that God would give her strength. She prayed that she would survive this ordeal. She prayed that she would figure out a way to escape. She prayed for Esperanza to come and save her.

"And lead us not into temptation, but deliver us from evil."

Deliver us from evil.

For Legs, that part of the prayer had taken on a whole new meaning.

Chapter

12

Dressed in a two-button, midnight black Calvin Klein suit and black Lauren shirt open at the collar, Esperanza looked sharp as he sauntered into Club Habanero. His polished John Lobb double-buckled monk shoes were extremely comfortable; hand finished, calf leather. He made his way through the dense crowd. Though the joint usually featured live Cuban music, it was tango night.

His eyes swept across the club. Romantic lighting. Oak columns. Velvet drapes.

Stylishly dressed couples glided across the polished teak floor, dancing to the live sextet crammed onto the tiny stage. Violins wailed. Accordion wept. Very close *abrazo*. Embrace. Mostly Anglo Americans and Argentines. Esperanza confidently made his way to the horseshoe-shaped bar, ordered a mojito, and admired the dancer's elegant and sultry moves.

Esperanza's mother Ramona was an accomplished dancer in an assortment of Latin American styles, from rumba to mambo to paso doble. She taught him the tango when he was in his early teens but he didn't really keep up with it; danced once or twice over the years, but that was it. As Esperanza sipped the minty-sweet mojito, his eyes continued to search every corner of the club. He could feel the vein in his neck throbbing. It was difficult for him to get control of his anger. Esperanza's eyes stopped when he spotted a man with slicked-back white hair dancing with a woman in a black silk dress. She had spectacular legs and was six feet tall.

Devona.

All he wanted was to walk up and shoot her in the head. Like that was going to happen.

Her cheek and upper body were pressed tight against the man as her endless, sinewy legs did searing *ganchos*, kicking and hooking around her partner's body. Devona was quite skillful and her movements extremely seductive. If the smiling man only knew that he was dancing with the devil, he'd run for the nearest exit.

Devona noticed Esperanza watching her and grinned.

Keep cool, Nick. Don't let her play you.

The song finished and the white-haired man dipped Devona with a dramatic flair and then she kissed him on both cheeks. *How European of her.*

A new song began. Women sat in their seats as men strutted back and forth checking them out. Some women lowered their heads, turning down their suitors, while others made eye contact, confirming their willingness to dance. Ironically, as elegant and sophisticated as the tango was, it had originated in the brothels of Argentina nearly a century ago. It was the way in which the johns solicited the prostitutes. The mating ritual remained virtually the same after all these decades, except now, it was a formal part of the dance.

Of course, Devona turned the tables on tradition and

strutted back and forth, a resourceful predator stalking prey. There wasn't a man or a woman in the joint who lowered their head when she walked by. They were all completely willing to be devoured by her.

Devona sashayed over to Esperanza and held her hand out, palm up. The other potential dance partners appeared disappointed by her selection.

"What?" Esperanza said.

"You're not going to refuse a woman a dance, are you? That would be extremely ungentlemanly."

For a second, Esperanza imagined himself strangling the witch. Instead, he graciously took her hand and guided her to the center of the dance floor.

A new tango song began. A slower, more sensual one. He pulled her into an *abrazo*, held her close and began to dance. At first, his movements were slightly awkward, but it all started coming back and he danced with a simple yet confident grace. Esperanza did a forward *ocho* and Devona followed in perfect synch with him. As a young man, he didn't appreciate the sultriness of tango. Now it was a whole different story. The music intensified as their feet moved to the pounding of the piano. It amazed Esperanza that such a vile creature as Devona emanated such alluring femininity.

The sweet vanilla scent of her hair, her supple breasts crushed against his chest, her soft, damp cheek pressed against his, her hot breath blowing on his ear, all sent his mind reeling. And this was only the first song of three he'd have to dance with her. *Jesus*.

Esperanza paused. Devona brushed her nose against his face and executed an agile *gancho*. With her leg hooked around his thigh, she whispered in his ear.

"Not bad. Didn't think you had it in you."

"I'm beside myself."

"You know what the name of this song is? 'Tango de la Venganza.' "

Revenge Tango.

Perfect.

"Are we gonna talk or what?"

"After this dance is done."

Devona performed elaborate *caricias*—caresses—seductively stroking her silk-stocking leg against the back of his thigh, calf, and inner thigh.

Backward step, side step and cross, then Esperanza danced backward, doing an *arrastre*, dragging Devona along the dance floor.

He pulled her into an *abrazo* once again, arm hooked around her back, the palm of his hand firmly planted on her ribs, right underneath her breast, and they both performed syncopated rhythmic footwork: stepping, sliding, and gliding. Drawing circles on the floor with the tips of their shoes. Noses and cheeks sensuously brushing against each other. So much intimacy expressed in such a public environment.

"This is why I love tango," she said over the sizzling violins as she subtly rubbed her breasts against his chest and her knee between his legs. Though Esperanza tried to resist her, he was turned on and got hard. Devona gazed at him, her wicked eyes declaring, *You're mine whether you like it or not. I own you.*

Closing his eyes and taking a deep breath, Esperanza fought back the urge to strangle her right there on the dance floor. Hate and desire made for a dangerous and volatile combo. It wasn't time yet. He had to be patient.

In the upstairs lounge, a fireplace roared as couples huddled on plush velvet love seats, talked, caressed, and kissed. Esperanza and Devona were in a cozy alcove in the rear, dark except for a single fluttering candle. She appeared relaxed, her arm draped around his shoulder as he sat beside her, stiff and somewhat distracted.

"You look awfully yummy tonight, Nick."

Her lustful gaze swept over him and his chest tightened. For a moment, it seemed as if he was unable to breathe.

"Can we cut the crap and get down to business?" he said.

She pouted. "No fun."

"I figured you might be a little more concerned about the fact that someone wants to put a bullet in your head, instead of playing your usual games."

She pulled her arm away and rested her head back against the love seat, gazing up at the shadows dancing on the ceiling.

"Fine. These are the rules. You go to the cops for help? Legs dies. You go to your FBI brother? Legs dies." She stared at him again. This time her eyes were cold and lifeless. "You double-cross me in any way? Legs dies. That clear enough?"

"Crystal. How do I know she's safe after the first phone call?"

"I'll arrange for you to have a brief chat every once in a while. Okay? But focus on the task at hand."

"Which is?"

"One: keeping me alive. Two: find out who put the hit on me. And . . ." She sensuously caressed the side of her neck.

"Three?"

"Kill them."

"What?"

"Come on, Esperanza. Don't play coy." She took a sip

of her chardonnay. "You think you'd find out who the culprit is, tell me, and that's it?"

"I'm not a killer—"

She cackled. "Don't fuckin' humor me. You had no problem killing my husband."

"That was self-defense."

"You lie to yourself like that?"

"Besides, Rybak deserved what he got."

Her lips tightened and her cheeks flushed. It was her eyes that frightened Esperanza. They turned into slits and bored into him, like being cut by a serrated blade. He realized he'd made an incredibly stupid mistake.

Devona gritted her teeth. "I'm the last girl in the world you wanna piss off, you know."

Esperanza knew he better back off. Legs's life was at risk, so he had to let Devona be in control.

"I'm sorry."

"Sorry?"

She angled forward, patiently waiting for him to answer.

Though it was incredibly difficult for him to say the words, which seemed to be stuck in his throat, they finally came out sounding like a hiss.

"I'm sorry, Mistress Love," he said and lowered his head in submission.

She patted him hard on the cheek. "That's a good slave."

Even with her life in danger, Devona was relentless when it came to being in control. Esperanza took a moment to pull it together, to stay on point. He raised his head and was careful not to express any defiance whatsoever.

"Do you have any leads for me? Any idea who might be after you?"

"Not a clue," she said with a casual shrug of the shoulders. "A couple of nasty dreadlocks came after me."

"Jamaicans?"

"Yeah. Sloppy. A dumbass drive-by attempt. One of 'em is dead. One got away. Vehicle was a black Ford Bronco."

"Remember a partial plate at least?"

"236VUD."

Esperanza pulled a small leather journal and a Caran d' Ache Varius blue lacquer fountain pen from his jacket pocket and scribbled notes in flowing letters.

"Nice pen. You do have damn fine taste. And it's sure cute to see you in detective mode." Devona dipped her index finger in the glass of wine and then provocatively sucked on it and added, "My own private dick."

He ignored the comment. "Anything else?"

"Another hitter came after me. A pro. His name is . . . *was* Cole Blue. I interrogated him and he told me that some Brooklyn wiseguy named Richie Goteri contracted him. He thought Goteri was only an intermediary, though."

"Anybody in Brooklyn you've pissed off recently that comes to mind?"

"I've traveled the world. But Brooklyn isn't my destination of choice."

"Come on, Devona. There's gotta be something you remember . . . solid lead you can give me to work with."

"If I had a solid lead, stud, I wouldn't need your help."

"Well, I'll see what I can dig up on the license plate for the Jamaican and background on Goteri. Take it from there."

"Who would've thought?"

"What?"

"Nicholas Esperanza and Mistress Devona Love teaming up."

He grabbed her hand and gently held it, though he really wanted to crush it. Hear the bone snap. Watch her cry out in agony. "Let me make something very clear, Devona," Esperanza said. "You harm Legs in any way, I'll make you suffer in ways worse than you've made so many others suffer."

She jerked her hand away and said, "The thing is, Nicholas"—she bent forward, hands clutching his thighs, face close to his, eyes turning dead calm—"I know you're quite capable of *anything.*"

Devona grabbed him by his crotch and aggressively stroked him but he managed to stay cool. Still got hard, though.

Bitch.

"As much as I enjoy your charming company, time for you to get to work and do what you do best." She gave him one last, painful squeeze and then leaned back, her expression nice and relaxed. "I'll call you in a few hours for an update."

Chapter

13

The GPS tracking device showed Devona's car going west on Eightieth street. Justice and Havelock had waited for Devona to come out from the club. As she was about to get into her rental car, an inconspicuous Saturn, Justice kept her occupied for a few seconds, asking her about what clubs to go to. Havelock snuck up, slid under the car, and placed the magnetic tracker on the vehicle's undercarriage and slipped away without being noticed.

Havelock was behind the wheel of his Lexus SUV while Esperanza sat in the passenger seat staring at the video screen of the handheld tracking device.

While they followed Devona, Justice did a search on the Saturn. It was rented to a dummy corporation called Torture Garden Enterprises. Justice tried to find out more about the company and who was behind it, but the tracks led to other dummy corporations and bank accounts in the Caymans. No single person tied to anything.

"Damn, this bitch is good," Justice said from the back seat as he closed the laptop. "Couldn't get anything on her." He leaned forward and looked over Esperanza's shoulder. "She knows how to stay invisible."

"That she does, when she wants to," Esperanza said.

They'd been tailing Devona's car for about twenty minutes.

"She's moving really erratically," Justice said. "Uptown, then down. West, then east."

"That's not a good sign," Esperanza said.

"Maybe she's making sure she's not being followed," Havelock said.

Esperanza's stomach churned. "Or she's made us."

"I Will Survive" chimed from Esperanza's pocket. He pulled out the cell phone and answered.

"Nick, Nick, Nick, Nick. Why you gotta be a dick?" Devona said. "You're tracking a cab. I should cut off Legs's pinky finger and FedEx it to you."

"No, wait. I'm sorry, Mistress." Esperanza's voice cracked. "I fucked up. I'm begging you, Mistress. Please, don't hurt her."

Long pause. Way too long.

"You got twelve hours to come up with a solid lead or I bring out a pair of wire cutters."

She hung up and Esperanza knew that from this moment on, he had to completely play by Devona's rules. Any other mistakes like this one, and Legs would end up paying with her life.

"How did she know we were tracking her?" Esperanza said as he flipped the phone closed. He hesitated a moment, then put the cell in the glove compartment. "The goddamn phone has to be bugged."

"So she's known our every damn move," Havelock said.

"Smart bitch," Justice said.

Esperanza suddenly exploded and slammed the back of his fist against the passenger side window severals times until the glass cracked and his knuckles were bleeding.

He caught his breath, looked at the smear of blood on the window, and said, "Head back to the club."

Devona clicked off the cell. Her eyes had been locked with Legs's the whole time she spoke to Esperanza. Legs never even flinched when Devona made the threats. She sat with her arms folded across her chest and an expression of rebelliousness on her lovely face. She was making Devona wet.

Esperanza didn't keep his word, why should I? Why not have a little fun now that he broke the rules?

Devona took a couple of leisurely steps forward.

"Better pray Esperanza comes through for you, baby doll."

"He will."

"Such confidence in your man. I remember what that feels like. But Esperanza took that away from me."

"Well, maybe if your husband wasn't trying to kill him."

"I'm not sure if you're really tough, or plain stupid. You don't seem to realize the jam that you're in."

"Trust me, I do."

Devona reached under her dress and pulled out a tiny silver Derringer from her leather thigh holster. She aimed the pistol at Legs.

"Stand up." She did. "Take off your clothes."

Legs appeared confused. "What?"

"You heard me." It was time for a lesson in discipline. Payback for Esperanza's double-cross. Devona was happy Esperanza gave her a reason to play. Legs was this appetizing dish she'd been waiting to consume, and now the opportunity had come.

Legs stripped down to her silk underwear. Devona's breathing practically turned into a pant as she admired

Legs's soft, sensuous curves. Skin the color of copper. Slim waist dipped into wide hips. Devona loved the voluptuous bodies of Latin women.

Legs unhooked her bra and tossed it to the floor. Devona's body started to tingle in anticipation. A fire raged between her thighs. Her mouth watered. As Legs finally removed her panties and stood there in all her naked glory, Devona thought about all their endless chats. How Legs opened up to her, shared her deepest secrets and let herself be completely vulnerable. Devona actually developed genuine feelings of kinship. It was probably the most intimate relationship she'd experienced with a woman who wasn't her lover. Devona cared for Legs. Thought she was very special.

Too bad her boyfriend was Nicholas Esperanza.

Too bad she had to pay the price.

Chapter
14

In his office at Sueño Latino, Esperanza hovered over Justice, who was behind the desk working on a laptop, doing a search of the NYPD's criminal database. At first, Esperanza was going to call Santos, but figured it was a bad idea. It might piss Devona off and Santos would start asking too many questions. Luckily, Justice managed to get access, just like he said he would.

Justice also disabled the bug in the cell phone. Though it was taking a chance, Esperanza figured Devona wasn't going to ask about it. If she did, Esperanza would claim ignorance. He needed the phone so she could communicate with him, but that was it. There was no way they'd be able to operate with her listening in and knowing their every move.

"Got it," Justice said and hit the Print button.

Esperanza raced over to the printer and pulled a rap sheet. The vehicle was registered to Vincent Notice. 2377 Nostrand Avenue. Born in Kingston, Jamaica. Raised in Crown Heights, Brooklyn. Thirty-two years old. Married. Pinched a bunch of times for possession of cocaine and marijuana with intent to sell. No assaults. No attempt at murder raps. Just a small-time drug dealer.

Havelock sauntered into the office. He wore a long leather coat, gloves, and carried an oversized canvas duffel bag. "Where are we headed?"

"Crown Heights."

"Home sweet home."

Havelock's Lexus sped around the majestic circle at Grand Army Plaza, past Prospect Park, past the Brooklyn Public Library, and on to Eastern Parkway.

Inspired by the boulevards of Berlin and Paris, Eastern Parkway was built in the late 1800s. The parkway had a central roadway, a grassy median with blooming trees and park benches lining pedestrian paths on each side, and a service road.

Eyes focused on the road, Havelock gunned the Lexus and swerved in and out of the dense traffic. Esperanza rode shotgun. The duffel bag was on his lap. He unzipped it. Inside, there were several automatic pistols, boxes of ammunition, and a couple of flash grenades.

Justice was sitting in the back, staring out the window, chewing on his thumbnail. Esperanza noticed he seemed to be a bit jittery. He knew Justice was quite good at tracking down bail jumpers and bringing them in. But how many serious firefights had he actually been involved in? Getting to the Jamaican might be a cakewalk or could turn into a full-fledged gun battle if he was a part of a drug gang. The Jamaican drug posses had ruled a large part of Brooklyn for the past couple of decades. They were known to be ruthless and crazy and trigger-happy. Firing machine pistols into a crowded street was as common to them as smoking blunts.

Esperanza loaded a 9mm Beretta semiautomatic and

passed the weapon to Justice, who took it, made sure the safety was on, and stuffed it in the waistband of his jeans.

"We need him alive. Remember that," Esperanza said.

"I'll follow your lead, yo," Justice said.

"You sure you okay with this?"

"Yeah, man. I got your back."

After searching through the duffel, Esperanza chose a Sig Sauer, his weapon of choice, and proceeded to load it. He glanced at Havelock, whose face was calm and determined.

They were a couple of blocks from Brooklyn Avenue. A thick fog had settled low to the ground. Endless crews of Hasidic Jews, looking identical in black suits, fedoras, trench coats, and bushy beards, strolled along the parkway's pedestrian walkway, fog swirling at their feet.

"Shit's surreal, yo," Justice said. "Reminds me of that movie *Dark City*."

Havelock made a right on Brooklyn Avenue and stopped at a red light. Esperanza stared at the regal church across the street and thought about Legs. He hoped she was okay. His eyes followed a gaggle of young, pretty Hasidic women as they crossed the street. They wore short bolero jackets and ankle-length denim skirts, which were tight around their broad hips and slit high up the back, revealing knee-high leather boots.

"Those Hasidic bitches sure got some juicy asses," Justice said. "The long skirt actually makes 'em look sexier. Since you grew up around here, Have, ever tap one of them?"

"Closest I ever came was a Jehovah's Witness," Havelock replied and then glanced at Esperanza. "How you holdin' up, E?"

"Fine," Esperanza said, even though Justice's constant chatter was getting on his nerves.

"How you wanna handle this?"

"Low key. We're gonna knock on the door and ask some questions."

They turned on President Street, which was lined with anorexic trees whose leaves were starting to sprout. On each side of the street there were elegant prewar brownstones painted beige or brown. Though it was late at night, Hasidic families were hanging out on stoops. A group of black kids played basketball.

Back in 1991, Crown Heights nearly burned down to the ground during the infamous riots sparked by a Hasidic man who had run down a Guyanese boy and his seven-year-old female cousin. A Hasidic ambulance showed up and the cops ordered them to take care of the driver instead of the kids. Longtime, simmering tensions between the Jews and the blacks finally exploded into violence. Black rage swept over the neighborhood: Cars were set afire. Bottles and rocks were thrown at cops in riot gear. Soon enough, an angry young black man determined to get payback stabbed a Hasidic student, who was visiting from Australia, to death.

Fortunately, in the past decade, the neighborhood managed to find an odd balance of cultures and races, which included West Indians, Jamaicans, African Americans, and Jews. Esperanza was amazed at how the city had transformed in the last fifteen years. But violence, poverty, and drugs were still alive and well in the Big Apple, no matter how polished it was.

Havelock parked in front of the only beaten-down brownstone on the block. Cracked façade. Peeling beige paint. Lopsided steps.

A group of tough-looking young black men were hanging out across the street in front of a deli, faces concealed by the oversized hoodies pulled over their heads. They were passing around a forty-ounce in a paper bag and suspiciously eyed Havelock's expensive vehicle.

Esperanza slipped the 9mm into his hip holster and got out of the SUV.

Chapter

15

Devona made sure the wrist suspension cuffs were securely in place. The restraints were made of leather and featured large metal rings that Devona clipped to a chain, which dangled from one of the cage's overhead bars.

Legs's arms were held high over her head and she was naked. She knew that Devona could've made the cuffs painfully tight but didn't.

What is Devona going to do to me? How far is she going to go?

Devona slipped a soft leather collar around Legs's neck. Metal rings clinking, a dog's leash clipped to the front ring, right under Legs's chin.

"Can you breathe okay?" Devona asked politely.

"Yeah. Look, Devona—"

"Shh." Devona was wearing latex elbow-length gloves and she placed her index finger to Legs's lips. Tugged on the leash. "Don't speak unless I tell you to." Devona had undergone a complete transformation. Shiny black latex thigh-high boots with four-inch stilettos and a matching corset from which her breasts provocatively spilled, replaced the cute cocktail dress she wore earlier. Her smooth, round bottom was bare.

Devona circled Legs, occasionally reaching out and caressing different parts of Legs's naked body. Stomach. Breast. Small of the back. Elbow. She stopped and faced Legs, her body an inch away. Devona's skin generated heat. Legs thought about kneeing her in the groin but knew that would be foolish. It would piss her off and make things much worse. She needed to play along, give Devona what she wanted, and maybe she'd get through this situation relatively unscathed.

"Kiss me," Devona ordered.

Though it went against her instincts, Legs reluctantly obeyed and closed her eyes and kissed Devona, fighting the feelings of disgust and hatred. Then she made her mind go blank and the kiss intensified as Devona slithered up and down, her gloved hands lightly tracing the curves of Legs's body. Devona pulled away and smiled, her lips gleaming with saliva.

Devona moved to Legs's left side, hooked her left arm around Legs's waist, and held her tight. Legs could feel Devona's clean-shaven pubic mound against her hip. She was searing wet. Shivers chased up Legs's spine and she shuddered.

"Arch your back."

Legs hesitated, until Devona roughly jerked the chain connected to the collar. As soon as Legs complied, Devona gave her a firm slap on the ass. Again. Then she lovingly caressed the places where Legs's skin stung and nibbled on her ear.

"Say, *Spank me, Mistress Love.*"

Legs wanted to spit in Devona's face and tell her to fuck off.

She said, "Spank me, Mistress Love."

"That doesn't sound very convincing."

Devona spanked her again, this time with much more force. The sting made Legs wince.

"Spank me, Mistress. Harder!"

Devona spanked and caressed and kissed her and Legs submitted to the pain, followed by pleasure, then pain again. Legs begged for more. She was ashamed at hearing herself say those words, but this was about survival, not pride.

Devona's sex juices trickled down Legs's thigh as the dominatrix continued undulating, swaying and grinding against her.

Legs closed her eyes. Her mind was reeling. She no longer felt disgust. Or even anger. Only confusion.

Am I surrendering because I don't want to be viciously tortured and maybe killed? Or am I surrendering because it feels good? Why is there a fire in my belly and I feel myself getting wet? Devona seems to know my body, what pleases me. The way she touches me, the way she kisses me, it's exquisite. No, Legs. Don't let her do this to you. Don't let her seduce you for real. Keep pretending.

Devona backed away. Legs opened her eyes. The dominatrix was leaning against the cage, her hands stuffed between her thighs as she eagerly fingered herself. She bit her bottom lip, her lust-filled eyes glued to Legs.

"You know how bad I could hurt you, right?"

"Yes."

"I have all kinds of whips and flogs and paddles," Devona said in a raspy voice. "I could burn you with cigarettes. Perform electrical genital torture."

Legs's heart beat out of control but she refused to show any fear. She'd be strong. Maybe it was time for her to take control. Maybe Devona wasn't as immune to emotion as she'd like to think.

"But you won't," Legs said.

Devona brushed hair away from her eyes and let out a throaty laugh.

"And why's that?"

"Because despite the fact that you were playing a part all these months, you have a genuine connection with me." Legs wasn't sure if she was right, she was trusting her gut and taking a chance. By the way Devona touched her, kissed her, Legs's female intuition told her it wasn't just a sexual thing. There was something deeper. There was emotion behind it. Sure, at any moment she could flip out and make Legs suffer agonizing pain. But right now, it was as if Devona needed to be close to her. "Come here," Legs said.

The smile vanished from Devona's face. Her visage went completely stoic, her body motionless and her gaze ice.

Legs shuddered as she wondered if she'd made a terrible mistake. Devona rushed over and let out an animalistic, ear-piercing shriek, and Legs jerked her head back. A series of expressions played across Devona's face: hatred, rage, sadness, desire, and even confusion. *She's open.* Legs counted the seconds until Devona's expression finally turned tranquil. She was ready.

"Now what?" Devona asked.

"Hold me," Legs said.

Havelock rang the bell several times. No answer. Esperanza stood behind Havelock and glanced over his shoulder. The homeboys across the street were still eyeing them. Because of their tough-guy posturing, Esperanza got the feeling they were packing heat under those hoodies. Justice was behind the wheel of Havelock's vehicle with the motor running. With the audience across the street, they couldn't pick the lock of the front gate.

Esperanza was growing impatient. They needed to get to Vincent quick. The clock was ticking. Havelock leaned on the bell some more.

Finally, a young Jamaican girl stuck her head out the second-floor window. She rubbed sleep from her eyes with the palm of her hands and let out a big yawn.

"Whachu want?"

"Lookin' for Vincent," Havelock said and flashed his killer smile. He spoke to her in a Jamaican accent.

"He ain't here."

"Know where I can find 'im, baby girl?"

"Why should I tell you?"

Havelock whipped out a wad of hundred dollar bills and held them up. "T'ing is, I owe 'im dis money and he's gonna be all pissed if I don't get it to him tonight."

The girl vacillated for a moment, and then said, "He's at the garage."

Devona pulled Legs close, methodically searched her eyes, and waited. Legs wanted to turn away from the powerful gaze, which almost made her tremble in fear.

Give the bitch what she wants. Make her believe she owns you. But what she really wants is to connect.

She leaned forward and kissed Devona. Delicately, her lips and tongue filled with longing.

Legs knew deep in her heart that what Devona needed at the moment was intimacy. Her yearning for her dead husband made Devona vulnerable, and Legs needed to take advantage of that. Their kissing grew more passionate, and their bodies rose and fell, rose and fell, silky warm female flesh pressing and sliding as they lost themselves to an increasingly fervent erotic dance.

This is the only way. If Devona senses any dishonesty, I'm gonna be in deep trouble. So I have to surrender to these feelings and let them be real.

Devona quivered as she rubbed her clit against Legs's clit, and her grinding intensified yet became more rhythmic. Legs imagined Sister Terez comforting her when she was so depressed she couldn't stop crying and Sister Terez held her in her arms, kissed her cheek, and stroked her hair. Such tenderness. Such love.

Devona buried her face in Legs's neck and cried out as she climaxed. She jerked her hips back and forth, and then made small circles with her hips, pubic mounds rubbing together, hot and wet and so, so sweet. Though Legs tried to fight it, her body seemed to have a mind of its own and an orgasm snuck up on her. Their bodies tensed, then shook and jerked as they let out cries of pleasure and lost themselves in their shared moment of ecstacy.

After a while, their bodies relaxed, their breathing grew deeper and deeper, and Devona squeezed Legs tightly.

I don't believe this shit. She made me come. How can she do that? How could I let myself? Why did it feel so fucking good? This is crazy. Absolutely crazy.

Devona untangled herself and stepped back, strands of damp hair stuck to her sweat-covered face. She brushed her hair back and sighed.

Then she slapped Legs with such force that Legs's head whipped to the side.

Though she was stunned for a moment, the salty taste of blood in her mouth snapped Legs from her trance and she flew into a rage and attempted to kick Devona, who easily sidestepped and then rammed her fist into Legs's stomach. Legs's body went slack and she gagged and fought to catch her breath, which at the moment seemed impossible.

"You think you're fucking cute? Huh? Appeal to my girly, sensitive side? A little love and affection?" Devona paced back and forth, hands waving around. "You're fucking sexy, and you genuinely surrendered, which is what got me off." Devona stopped pacing, came closer, and raised her hand to strike again, and Legs flinched. "See? That reaction? That's what *really* turns me on. *Fear.* The only thing that's keeping me from torturing you right now is that I gave my word. But if Esperanza doesn't deliver something solid by tomorrow?" Devona forced her hand between Legs's clamped thighs and roughly fingered her. Legs didn't bother fight it. She was too busy trying to breathe. "You're going to experience such agony and humiliation, you'll eventually beg me to kill you."

Devona pulled her hand away, spit in Legs's face, and marched out of the cage, disappearing into the darkness.

Though she desperately didn't want to, Legs began to cry. Since her body was limp, her weight was bearing down on the leather cuffs and it made her wrists hurt. She straightened up and balanced herself as she choked back tears. Legs couldn't believe she was naïve enough to think that she could possibly manipulate a sadistic sociopath like Devona. Instead, she'd made a complete fool of herself by submitting to the dominatrix. She felt humiliated. Ashamed.

Which is exactly what Devona wanted her to experience.

Legs went berserk. She jerked on the chain, kicked at the air, and screamed until she was completely exhausted. She hung there and lowered her head. Didn't matter that her wrists ached or that her face still stung. At least she was still alive.

You did what was necessary to survive. You bought yourself some time. Don't question what you felt. It's done. The only thing that matters is staying in one piece so that Nick can come and get you the fuck out of here.

Chapter

16

The garage was a squat, one-story red brick building that looked like a bunker. It was sandwiched between a local bar called Sparky's and an ugly ten-story apartment complex. Metal shutters covered in colorful graffiti were pulled down. There was a long, narrow alley between the apartment complex and the garage.

In the junk-strewn alley, under the cover of darkness, Havelock immediately got to work on the garage's side door lock, while Esperanza and Justice kept watch. It had been many years since Havelock picked a lock. Took exactly five seconds. *Click*. Havelock opened the steel door and they silently slipped into the garage, guns drawn. Esperanza took the lead, moving quickly and silently, gun hand held straight forward. Loud dancehall reggae was emanating from inside the garage accompanied by the sound of men laughing and the intoxicating smell of marijuana.

And gasoline.

Esperanza, Havelock, and Justice hid behind a van. It was a fairly spacious garage. There were at least five vehicles in various states of repair. A couple of dismantled engines. Stacks of tires. Havelock peeked through the driver's side window of the van. So did Esperanza.

Under harsh fluorescent lights, a man in grease-covered coveralls was tied to a wooden chair. He was soaked. Badly beaten and a bloody mess. Havelock recognized Vincent from his mug shot. There was an oily rag stuffed in his mouth.

There were two other brothers. Both sported long dreadlocks and both were shirtless. Decorating their muscular bodies were a variety of elaborate tattoos. One of them had an automatic tucked in the waistband of his jeans. The other loosely held an Uzi submachine gun at his side. They laughed and passed a huge blunt and a bottle of Jamaican rum back and forth as they watched a third man sodomize a black woman on the cement floor. She was heavyset and dark skinned, her wrists were tied behind her back with a rope, and her jeans and panties were pulled down around her ankles. Her cheek was pressed against the floor in a pool of her own saliva and her eyes stared vacantly while the man clutched her wide hips and viciously raped her from behind.

Havelock wasn't going to feel an ounce of remorse taking these lowlifes out.

Vincent wept and attempted to look away. There was a gash on his temple and his left eye was practically swollen shut. His nose was bashed to a pulp and his lips were split open and oozing blood. The Jamaican with the Uzi picked up a can of gasoline and poured it over Vincent's head. Vincent shook violently and let out muffled cries.

"We gonna fuck yer wife till she dead, mon," the Rasta said and dropped the empty gas can on the floor. "Then we gonna burn ya alive."

Havelock glanced over at Esperanza, who signaled for Havelock to go left and for Justice to go right, flanking him, while he went straight down the middle. He nodded and Havelock and Justice quietly crept away, using other vehicles as cover.

Except Esperanza didn't wait; he strolled out from behind the van and walked straight ahead, pistol aimed. *Goddamn cowboy.* Havelock didn't like it when Esperanza took unnecessary risks.

All the men froze for a moment, obviously wondering who the hell Esperanza was, and then went for their weapons. Esperanza shot the one with the Uzi in the forehead. Blood spurted from between his eyes and he dropped to the ground. Havelock emerged from the left. The second man reached for his automatic. Havelock nailed him twice in the chest. The impact of the 9mm slugs knocked him back. He stood there for a moment, staring down at the blood spurting from the large bullet holes, then fell face forward.

The rapist froze, still on top of the catatonic woman.

"Don't shoot, please," he said as he leapt off her and stood up, his hands held high over his head.

Justice trotted over and pistol-whipped the rapist, sending him reeling backward. Then he aimed the weapon at the Jamaican's head and said, "Make a move, Rasta mon, and I'll blow your fuckin' brains out."

Esperanza calmly strolled up to the disoriented rapist and delivered a powerful kick to his bare crotch. The man howled, dropped to his knees, and then rolled on the floor, hands holding on to his precious jewels. Then Esperanza went berserk and kept on kicking and kicking the hell out of him.

Havelock shook his head. Esperanza was letting rage

get the better of him and it could become a problem.
He'd have to have a talk with him a little later. Time to
take care of business. Havelock stepped over to Vincent
and pulled the rag from his mouth. The stench of gasoline was overwhelming. Justice covered up the naked
woman with a coat and checked her pulse.

"Mary!" Vincent wailed.

"Are you, Vincent?" Havelock asked.

"Mary!"

Esperanza slapped Vincent across the face and made
him snap out of it. "You're Vincent Notice, right?"

"Yeah . . . yeah."

Esperanza leaned over and stared in Vincent's dis-
traught eyes. "Who are these pricks?"

"King's men."

"Who's King?"

"He be my boss."

"Was he the one who sent you after Devona?"

Vincent appeared even more perplexed. "Who?"

"The white woman you tried to kill in an underground
garage in Manhattan. The woman who took out your
partner?"

"Untie me."

"After you answer my questions."

"But my wife . . ."

Esperanza grabbed Vincent's battered face and
squeezed. Hard. Though Havelock knew that Esperanza
felt bad about what happened to Mary, it wasn't his concern at the moment. Saving Legs was.

"After you answer my questions."

"Okay, okay . . . King ordered us to kill 'er." Vincent's
Jamaican accent was pretty heavy, and Havelock noticed
Esperanza had to pay close attention to decipher the

words. He got most of it. "But we fucked up. He gave me another chance but I couldn't track da bitch down. So he sent dese men to make an example of me 'cause he don't tolerate failure."

"How did he know where to find her?"

"Dunno."

"King's a drug dealer?"

"Big time," Vincent said between pants. "Runs the Voodoo Blood Posse."

That moniker was familiar to Havelock. Straight out of Kingston, Jamaica, the Voodoo Blood Posse was one of the most notorious drug gangs in Brooklyn. Crack, coke, and weed. Controlled major territories in East New York, Bed Stuy, and Canarsie. Were famous for their preferred method of torture: burning their rivals alive, then setting fire to their rivals' families. Children. Grandmothers. *Everybody.* Narcotics and DEA had been trying to shut them down since the early nineties, but these maniacs instilled too much fear and it was impossible for undercover agents to infiltrate the gang and no one would ever dare testify against them.

"Where can I find him?"

"I dunno. Mary . . ." He wept, snot and blood running from his nose, saliva and blood running from his mouth.

Vincent was a mess. Wouldn't be of much use.

"Untie him," Esperanza said to Justice and then squatted, grabbed the rapist by his dreads, jerked his head back, and shoved the 9mm under his chin.

"What's your name, you degenerate piece of shit?"

"Razor," he said with a foolish mix of pride and arrogance.

"I'm gonna ask you once, Razor. Where do I find your boss, King?"

"I ain't telling ya shit."

"Gotta be a fuckin' hardcase, huh? Well, it's your funeral."

Esperanza's eyes scanned the garage. Havelock knew Razor was going to talk whether he liked it or not. There was an eight-foot-long wooden worktable with a heavy-duty bench vise attached to one of the corners. Esperanza dragged Razor by his hair to the table and threw him on top of it. "Hold him down," he said to Havelock.

Havelock understood what he needed to do. He put his gun away and placed Razor in a tight headlock. As soon as Justice untied Vincent, he ran over to his wife and took her in his arms. She didn't respond. She was hiding someplace deep in her own mind and might never return.

Razor struggled to get loose, but Havelock's grip was unbreakable. Esperanza stuffed his gun in his holster and then leaned close and stared at Razor with dead serious eyes. He grabbed the Rasta's wrist and placed his hand in the jaw of the vise.

"I'm gonna ask you one more time. How do I find King?"

"Fuck you."

"Wrong answer."

With all the strength he could muster, Esperanza spun the lever of the vise. There was a loud cracking sound as the metal jaw crushed Razor's hand and he shrieked for dear life.

From the corner of his eye, Havelock noticed a shocked Justice as he turned away in disgust. Cuz obviously didn't have the stomach to handle this kind of hard core situation.

Esperanza slapped Razor's face. He was crying now. Wasn't so tough anymore.

"You don't answer me, you lose your hand. Then the other hand. Then your fuckin' feet."

"Please, no . . . no . . . I'll tell ya whacha wanna know."

After Razor sang, high notes, low notes, everything he knew about King, without an ounce of remorse, Esperanza left him there, crushed hand still in the vise.

Esperanza stared at Vincent, eyes full of pity. Vincent was on the floor, weeping and cradling his catatonic wife. Esperanza handed Vincent one of the dead Rastafarian's guns and said, "Do what you gotta do."

While walking down the alleyway, they heard two gunshots. Havelock figured Vincent finished off Razor. Justice, walking next to Havelock while Esperanza sauntered ahead of them, leaned over and in a low voice said, "Your boy. He's on some John Woo shit. That nigga's scary, yo."

"His woman's life is on the line. You expect him to handle things with kid gloves?"

Havelock had a gut feeling this was coming. Though Justice had a great rep as a tracker and could handle himself in pretty touchy situations, he wasn't exactly known for serious gunplay. Things were about to get really ugly. This drug dealer King sounded like no joke. This was going to turn into commando work. It was easy for Havelock to predict that there was going to be a lot of dead bodies. And it was definitely more than Justice might be able to deal with.

"You can walk away, cuz. This isn't your fight."

"Ain't like I'm scared, Hav. But all the bail jumpers I've busted over the years, I ain't never had to shoot nobody. I got a wife and kids."

The situation would be bad enough if Esperanza got

out of control, Havelock didn't have the time to watch his cousin's back, too.

"It's cool, Justice. Nick and I can handle this."

"You two are gonna take on a whole Jamaican drug posse by yourselves?"

Havelock patted Justice on the back and grinned.

"We're an army of two, baby."

Chapter
17

Her hands and wrists were numb and she was dozing off. Legs was uncertain how long she'd been dangling inside the cage, but it seemed like hours. It was dark and the only sound was the constant drip of water from the overhead pipes.

Her body ached, exhaustion was setting in, and she badly needed to urinate. She wondered how long Devona was going to leave her hanging.

Leave me hanging. Literally. Ha, ha, ha. Funny.

Almost as if her mind needed to take her somewhere else, thoughts of the past suddenly appeared like comforting old family pictures and movies. Images of her and Esperanza sharing their first kiss. They were sitting on a warped bench in a park in El Barrio after playing a long game of handball, all sweaty and salty. The last rays of sunlight painted streaks of amber across the horizon. Boy, how she swooned, how her body became electric. That kiss was like some wonder drug that sent her on a trip of pure, sweet euphoria.

He was sixteen and she was fourteen. Legs had a major crush on him since she first moved to his block on 116th street when she was nine years old. But to him she was just a child. Esperanza was always friendly and talked to her, treated her like his little sister, and never teased her like the other kids did. They teased her because she was taller than all the girls and most of the boys in the neighborhood and was awfully scrawny until she turned thirteen. That's how she got the nickname Legs in the first place. Everybody assumed it was because of how she looked now, but her aunt, Titi Luz, gave her the nickname when she was six because her legs were so skinny that it looked like she was walking on stilts. The nickname stuck.

Then her body transformed overnight. All her spectacular curves seemed to appear out of nowhere. Of course, all the girls got jealous, and all the boys started to hit on her—except for Esperanza.

When Legs started high school, she was a freshman and Esperanza was a junior, and she finally convinced him to take her out on a date. She was smarter and much more mature than most of the other girls and he appreciated that confidence while the other boys were intimidated.

Months passed, and one night, while her parents were out at a dance at a local community center, Esperanza and Legs were sitting on the plastic-covered couch in her living room, passionately making out. Things got hotter and hotter until she finally offered a stunned sixteen-year-old Esperanza her virginity.

Much to her dismay, Esperanza said, "I want you, Legs. I'd love to be your first, but you ain't gotta do this. You know you're my heart. We can wait. As long as it takes." Those words made her love him even more and want him more, so she refused to take no for an answer.

He reluctantly relented, and though it was awkward

and a bit painful at first, Esperanza was patient and gentle and tender and it made the experience truly special. Unlike her friends, she didn't get quick-humped against a tree in the park and a "I'll see ya around, *mami*," kiss-off. Next day, the boy would brag all over school how he popped the girl's cherry.

Legs and Esperanza were together for three more years, until he enlisted in the Navy. After he shipped off to basic training, Legs was heartbroken for months and promised herself she'd wait for him. But while she was attending her first year of college as a business major, she met and fell in love with Stewart, a graduate student. White guy from the 'burbs. Well educated. It was so hard for her to write that "Dear Juan" letter to Esperanza, but she couldn't leave him hanging. He deserved better.

The first couple of years with Stewart were good, though the relationship never had the kind of passion that she experienced with Esperanza. Eventually the marriage started to go south as Stewart quickly became a hugely successful investment banker and was more dedicated to making money than to his marriage.

Her mother didn't understand what she was complaining about. "*Mira, mija*," she'd say. "You are twenty-two years old, live in a beautiful home, have three cars, fancy jewelry and clothes. You're living the American dream. So your husband doesn't pay you too much attention, so what? Welcome to the club. At least you'll never be on welfare, never need food stamps, never have to struggle to make ends meet."

When Legs would come to El Barrio to visit her parents, she'd run into Esperanza from time to time. They'd hang out and she always felt comfortable being around him. They were obviously still in love but their lives had taken completely different paths. Eventually, he joined the police force, married some crazy Dominican chick from the boogie-down Bronx, who made him miserable because she was mad jealous and constantly accusing him of banging every woman in sight, including Legs. It wasn't until years later, after Esperanza and Legs were both divorced and had developed a much more mature friendship, that they again hooked up romantically.

In many ways, deep down, Legs always believed that some day they'd be together. The timing was finally right. She could never imagine herself with any other man except for Nicholas. No one could ever make her happier. No one could ever make her feel more alive.

The basement lights suddenly came on, shocking Legs out of her stroll down memory lane. She squinted, eyes adjusting to the harsh brightness.

Otto stepped into the cage, carrying a washbasin and a washcloth. A towel was draped over his shoulder. He placed them on the floor, then went over to her and unclipped the binds. He smelled like baby powder. She struggled on wobbly legs and Otto helped her to the cot.

"Thank you," she said, massaging her sore wrists. Her hands were slightly blue from the lack of circulation.

"You're welcome."

He handed her the washcloth and held the basin as she washed her face. The warm water felt good.

"Why are you doing this?"

"Because Mistress ordered me to."

"You do everything she says?"

"I'm her slave," he said, sounding quite proud of the fact.

Legs searched his eyes. They exuded kindness and gentility, just like his voice. But Legs had no doubt that if Devona ordered him to snap her neck, Otto wouldn't hesitate to do so.

"Are you scared of her?"

"Yes. And I'm in love with her as well."

By the glint in his eye, Legs could tell he meant it.

"She doesn't love you."

"How do you know that?"

"The only man she loves is her husband."

"How do you know for sure?" His voice was sad. A touch of anger, too.

"I just do."

He handed her the towel and she dried her face. She rotated her neck, which was stiff from her nodding off.

"I shouldn't be speaking with you. But I will give you one piece of advice: Don't make the Mistress mad."

"Yeah. I kind of got that."

Devona suddenly appeared from behind Otto. She carried a bag from Starbucks. Otto collected the towel, washcloth, and basin and stepped away, but stood guard at the entrance of the cage.

She dangled the white paper bag like a treat for a pet, and said, "There's a cup of green tea, a latte, and a lovely assortment of cookies and muffins."

Though Legs wanted to tell her to go to hell, she wasn't going to take any more idiotic chances. Besides, she was cold, and definitely hungry. She needed to keep her strength up. Legs reluctantly took the bag from Devona, looked inside, and removed the cup of green tea.

"I hope it makes you feel a little better."

"Yeah . . . thanks."

Legs didn't want to look Devona in the eye. It was the only way to keep her emotions in check. She opened the lid of the cup, took in the tea's comforting aroma, and sipped it.

"Sorry about the outburst earlier," Devona said. "Not many people manage to piss me off so easily."

"I'm flattered."

"Oh, Legs, stop playing the hardcase broad, okay? Look at me." Legs did. To her surprise, Devona's expression was one of compassion, and it made Legs so uncomfortable, she found herself squirming.

"You're out of your element. If you do as you're told, you'll come out of this in one piece. Leave the tough stuff to Nicholas."

Legs noticed Devona had changed into an alluring lavender cat suit made of sumptuous velvet. Cute ankle boots with chunky three-inch heels and rugged side buckles. Her hair was tied in a ponytail. Very little make-up on her face. The dominatrix flashed a rueful smile.

"I've learned my lesson," Legs said. "Trust me."

"Good for you. I'm going to meet with Nicholas in a little while to discuss a couple of things. Behave yourself."

Legs lowered her gaze to the floor, demurely said, "Yes, Mistress," and then bit her bottom lip so hard, she tasted blood.

Chapter
18

As soon as Esperanza stepped out of the lobby of his building, the loud honk of a car horn startled him enough to make him reel around. Santos was behind the wheel of a dark blue Chevy sedan. He got out of the car and casually strolled over. It was obvious that he was off duty, since he was wearing a leather motorcycle jacket, brown fleece pullover, jeans, and running shoes. A Yankees cap was perched on his shaven head.

"Hey, Nicholas," Santos said, holding out his hand.

Esperanza was caught off guard. Took him a moment to shake Santo's hand.

"What are you doing here?" Esperanza said, probably sounding more apprehensive at his ex-partner's unexpected visit than he intended to.

"Just following up." A late-evening wind howled and Santos pulled up the collar of his leather jacket. "Left you a coupla messages but you haven't gotten back to me."

"Been a little busy."

Esperanza didn't have time for this. He was on his way to meet with Havelock to plan on how they were going to snatch King. The last thing he needed was Santos snooping around. He was also concerned that Devona might be watching him, and seeing him talking to his cop friend wouldn't be something she'd appreciate.

"Any updates on the Devona situation?"

"No," Esperanza said and wagged his head as a couple of rude New Yorkers walked between them without saying excuse me. "It's like she just gave up. Maybe something happened to her. Or maybe I was imagining things in the first place."

It annoyed Esperanza that he always had a difficult time lying to Santos, so he was never very convincing.

"That's pretty convenient." Santos looked up at Esperanza's building. "How's Legs?"

"She's fine."

Santos's inquisitive eyes met with Esperanza's. He wasn't buying any of the story. "I went by Sueño Latino to say hello and they told me she was on vacation."

"She needed a few days off. Not feeling so well. What's the big deal?"

"C'mon, Esperanza. Don't bullshit me."

Esperanza grabbed Santos by the sleeve of his leather jacket and dragged him to the entrance of his building, away from the pedestrian traffic. Time to nip this in the bud.

"Do me a favor, Santos," he said, voice stern. "Stay out of this."

"Out of what?"

"I can't talk about it. I'm your friend and ex-partner. I need you to trust me."

"I wanna help."

"You can't. You just being here is putting Legs's life in danger."

"Tell me what's going on."

"You want to risk your badge? Your career? Maybe even end up in jail?" Santos didn't reply. His expression remained stone cold. "Then stay out of it."

"C'mon, Nick."

Esperanza placed his hands on Santos's shoulders, fingers digging in as he squeezed hard. He leaned forward, the tip of his nose almost touching Santos's nose.

"I'm asking you as a friend. Let me handle this. Stay away."

Santos's eyes darted all over the place. He seemed to debate whether he should push things further. He stared back at Esperanza, his eyes filled with concern.

"I don't feel good about this, but I'll do as you ask. If you need help . . ."

A sense of relief washed over Esperanza. It surprised him that Santos was giving up so easily, but he didn't care, he had more important things to do.

"I know, Santos," Esperanza said and then kissed his friend on the cheek. "Trust me, I know."

Ella Fitzgerald was crooning "Cry Me A River." Esperanza sat in his Jaguar, parked on the corner of Broadway and Fiftieth Street listening to Ella's sultry voice and waiting for Devona. Every time Esperanza heard Ella sing, it gave him chills because it reminded him that such beauty could still exist in such a dark world.

The encounter with Santos earlier in the evening made him feel anxious. He hoped Santos would stay out of it as he promised and not let his cop instincts get the better of him.

The passenger door opened and Devona climbed in, carrying a leather shoulder bag. She had on a stylish black velvet cloak with a hood.

Esperanza's hands gripped the wheel tighter. He kept

his gaze straight out the window, giving himself a minute before looking at Devona. Otherwise he might hurt her. Hurt her bad.

"Nice ride," she said, pulling the hood down. "Drive."

He finally looked at her. "Where?"

"Around. I like the city at this time."

The Jag cruised uptown. It was almost dawn. The night sky was beginning to glow with streaks of rich amber light, and there was barely a soul walking the streets of midtown Manhattan. Devona turned up the stereo's volume. She sang for a minute. Actually had a lovely voice.

"I love Ella. She's fierce. Didn't peg you for a fan."

"'Cause of my father. I grew up listening to Ella and Dino and Frank."

"You're definitely a Sinatra kind of boy."

Esperanza was finding the small talk with Devona somewhat disconcerting but he figured it was best to play along with her.

"Yeah. I was a natural-born Rat Packer."

When they stopped at a red light, Devona magically produced a tiny glass vial with a metal spoon attached by a chain to the cap.

"You mind?"

"Knock yourself out."

Devona unscrewed the cap. Dipped the spoon in the yellowish powder. Sniff, sniff. She threw her head back and let out a growl.

"Want a hit?"

He debated. Feeling exhausted, he wouldn't mind a slight boost. But doing blow with Devona was probably a bad idea.

"I'm driving."

"So?"

She dipped the spoon in the vial, leaned over, and placed it under his nostril. Esperanza sniffed the coke. She did the other nostril. He sniffed again. Slight burn. Blast of energy straight to his brain. Vision became clear. Thinking became alert. Body was ready to fuck or fight. First hit of blow always lit up the senses quite nicely. *After that you start losing all sense and just want more and more.* She took another hit and put the vial away.

"By the way, how did you get the Jamaican to rat out his boss?"

"I put his hand in a vise."

"Ooh." She clapped and grinned vibrantly, her expression almost that of an excited ten-year-old girl. "You can be very persuasive when you want to."

"You know this hasn't exactly been a straight 'investigation.' Not exactly detective work," Esperanza said. "Shootings and dead bodies. And I got a feeling it's gonna get worse."

"You were expecting *Murder on the Orient Express*? You thought that while looking into hitters, drug dealers, and wiseguys you'd get to sit around asking questions and sipping port?"

"No, but—"

"So you get to bump off a few lowlife criminals. What's the downside? Sorry you ain't getting your whole homicide detective groove on, but it should appeal to that ruthless soldier part of you."

"Yeah. Fine," Esperanza said, keeping his eyes glued to the street. Welcome to Devona's world. "Before we discuss anything else, I want to talk to Legs."

"I figured so. Even going to let you see her. Pull over for a minute."

He parked the Jag in front of a Rite Aid pharmacy. Devona unzipped the shoulder bag and produced a laptop computer, placed it on her lap, turned it on, and waited for it to boot up. Connected her cell phone to it, typed, and then swiveled it around so he could see Legs on the screen, staring back him. Some kind of video conferencing.

"Nick?" Her voice sounded tinny coming through the laptop's small speakers.

His heart pounded against his chest, despite the overwhelming sense of relief at seeing that Legs was alive and well.

"You okay, baby?"

"Yeah."

"Has she hurt you?"

"No. I'm fine."

He wasn't sure if she was lying. She appeared haggard. Sounded a little distant. But if Devona had done something bad to her, Legs wouldn't be talking so calmly right now. She seemed to be in some kind of metal cage, but the lighting was too dim to make out any background details.

"I'm gonna get you out of there as soon as I can."

"I know." She gave him a weak smile.

The screen went black.

"Legs?"

Devona closed the laptop. Esperanza clenched his eyes shut for a moment and took a deep breath. *Stay in control, Nick. Don't piss Devona off.*

"You know she's fine, so let's get down to the biz," Devona said and put the laptop away.

Esperanza unbuckled his seat belt, swiveled around, and faced her. She rested the side of her face against the soft leather headrest and stared at him with rapacious eyes. Though her face was mostly concealed by eerie shadows, every once in a while a passing car's headlights would illuminate her. The effect was almost seductively cinematic.

"Havelock and I have hatched out a plan to get to King. It won't be easy. He's got a lot of firepower."

"Well, that's your thing, isn't it? I read up on the Navy SEALs. Precise. Ruthless. Deadly. Why did you become a run-of-the-mill cop when you were part of such an elite assault team?"

"Missed my family. Missed New York. Never intended to make the military my life."

"You know, you should really marry Legs. As much as she says it doesn't matter, it does."

Esperanza's body tensed up. Devona's off-the-cuff comment threw him for a loop. "I don't really want to discuss my relationship with Legs with you."

"Why not? I know all your intimate secrets. She and I were such close friends."

"I know how much you like games, but I'm not in the mood to play and we have more important things to deal with."

She pondered his response for a moment, shrugged, and then went back to the subject at hand. "So after you have a chat with this King, what's next?"

"Depends on what information I get out of him."

"Are you going to see Goteri?"

"He's a made guy. I want to take a more . . . diplomatic approach. I can't ask 'suspects' any questions if they're dead. I'm going to try and arrange an actual sit-down."

Her hazel eyes gleamed with perverse excitement and she ran her tongue over her scarlet-painted lips. "If you do, I want to go with you."

"That's not a good idea."

"You do as I say, remember?"

"Fine." Esperanza sniffed back the *perico*. Wished he

had a cigar and a glass of scotch. Wanted another damn hit of coke. "You're really good at this blackmail thing, aren't you?"

"Let's not call it blackmail. I prefer extortion. It's sexier."

"Tell me the truth. Why are these people after you?"

"I really have no idea, Nicholas."

She took his hand and tenderly caressed it. Played with his thick fingers. It sent chills up his spine. He fought back desire, then rage. With Devona, those two feelings always seemed to go hand in hand. Probably the way she liked it.

"Who are you?"

"What do you mean?" She coyly batted her eyelashes.

"What made you like this?"

"Want to know if I was an abused child or something?" She did a melodramatic pout, and then rested his hand on her firm thigh. The velvet was incredibly soft and Esperanza could feel her body heat. "I had a lovely middle-class upbringing on the West Coast. My father was an architect and my mom was an entertainment attorney. I decided I wanted to be an actress, much to their displeasure, and moved to New York when I was nineteen. Went to acting school. Went to countless auditions. Partied. A girlfriend of mine turned me on to the S&M scene. Loved it. I was a natural. Became a pro domme. Sure was better than being a waitress. Eventually gave up on the whole acting thing." She roughly pushed his hand away and stared out the windshield, and her expression turned gloomy. "A few years later I met Jason. Fell in love. We got married." Her voice quavered ever so slightly but seemed more like a scream of pain from a very tortured soul. "And he showed me a new way of life. Brought out the best in me." She turned back to him. For the first time, Devona actually appeared vulnerable. Not a side of her Esperanza ever expected to see. "That's it in a nutshell."

He wondered if any of the story was actually true. "Doesn't tell me much."

Vulnerability didn't last long.

"Don't try and sucker play me. I'm not going to reveal to you any substantial info. I know you want to find out my real identity, but it's not going to happen. The woman I once was died a long time ago."

"Whatever you say, Devona."

She slapped him across the cheek. It stung. He almost slapped her back.

Chill, Nicholas.

"Mistress."

"Mistress. Sorry."

"I'm not insane, you know."

"No. Never pegged you for crazy."

"What, then?"

"A sociopath."

"Cheesy. I prefer 'free spirit.' "

"If that makes you happy."

"Drop me off in Chelsea. I'm going to an after-hours party. You should probably get some sleep. Got a big day tomorrow."

He put the Jag in gear and peeled out. "That's a nice way of putting it."

"You know, Nicholas," she leaned over, rested her chin on his shoulder, "sometimes I wonder. What if we'd met under other circumstances?" Her fingers danced along his chest. "Both of us single. I'm sure it would've been quite an adventure."

The whole idea was so preposterous it made him laugh. Truth was, if Devona weren't a sociopath, if she weren't a predator, if she weren't the personification of evil, Esperanza would've probably fallen in love. And paid with his soul.

"As long as there was no torture and murder involved."

"Why take all the fun out of it?"

Chapter
19

Havelock switched on the overhead light of his private storage locker, revealing stacks of large aluminum cases.

"My personal armory," he said.

He flipped open one of the cases. It contained an M4 light machine gun. M203 grenade launcher. And a bunch of accessories, including a sound suppressor and a night-vision scope. Esperanza's eyes lit up. Havelock knew Esperanza kept a collection of automatics, but nothing approximating this impressive mini-armory.

Esperanza grinned. "This brings back memories."

"Well, I got all the gear we need. Standard weapon load-out."

"I'm glad you have all of this, but I have to wonder why."

"You know me, Nick. I like to be prepared for any contingency."

"I hear that." Esperanza held the M4 in his hand. Enjoyed the balance. Ran his fingers along the curves of the weapon. Havelock noticed that the touch was practically sexual. A boy and his guns. A shadow fell across

Esperanza's face. Looked like all the sadness and pain of the world were about to pour out of him. "I'm worried."

"That we won't pull this off?" Havelock opened another case. It contained a variety of grenades. Flash. Tear gas. Explosive. They could take down a small army if need be.

"Not that."

"What, then?"

"Let's say we find out who put this hit on Devona and take them down." Esperanza placed the machine pistol back in the case and gently closed it. "What if the bitch double-crosses me and kills Legs anyway?"

"Unfortunately, all you got is her word."

Esperanza began to pace while chewing on his thumbnail. Beads of sweat dotted his forehead. "That's not fuckin' good enough," he said as he shook his head.

Havelock carefully watched his friend. He was growing more and more concerned about Esperanza's abilities to handle what was to come. He was getting way too emotional, which could cause deadly mistakes on his part. Havelock understood that this was about Legs and how much Esperanza loved her, but that wasn't an excuse. The man was an emotional time bomb.

They'd both been trained to protect and to kill. And they were able to kill with detached efficiency. If they were going to pull this off, they needed to rely on their skills and training as SEALs. Emotions couldn't be a part of the equation.

As if on cue Esperanza lost it and began smashing his fists against the metal doors of the storage room. The growl he let out made Havelock shudder. The rage was coming from a deep, dark, endless pit, not something easy to control. The last thing Esperanza needed was broken bones in his hands.

Havelock grabbed him from behind in a bear hug. Esperanza fought like a crazy man to break free. He let Esperanza struggle for a minute, then let him go. When Esperanza turned around, Havelock slapped him so hard, he'd probably have a couple of loose teeth. Esperanza froze, completely stunned. Havelock slammed his forearm into Esperanza's throat and used his massive weight to pin him against the wall.

"You listen to me carefully, my brother. You're lettin' emotion get the best of you and you're gonna fuck up." Havelock pressed his forearm tighter against Esperanza's throat, completely cutting off his oxygen. "I know you don't want Legs to get hurt and I also know you got this thing . . . this rage with Devona. But if you don't start thinkin' like a soldier, a hunter, if you don't pull it together and get methodical, Legs is gonna die." Havelock could see the rage fading from Esperanza's eyes. "And Devona wins. You know I'll follow you anywhere, straight to hell, but not like this, partner. Don't turn this into no fool's errand."

Havelock released him and Esperanza doubled over and hacked up a gob of blood and phlegm. He stood up straight and stared at Havelock with calm, cool eyes. Eyes of a cold-blooded killer.

Now he was ready.

From the rooftop of the enormous three-story Brooklyn warehouse, Esperanza and Havelock staked out the dark, empty parking lot entrance, sweeping every inch of the area with tactical night-vision binoculars. They were dressed in black commando uniforms, wore light body armor, knit caps on their heads, and had a full complement of weapons at their disposal.

Esperanza thought about what had gone down at the

storage locker. He was glad Havelock had forced him out of his emotional spiral. He'd been losing all sense of control. Not anymore.

"You think Razor lied to us?" Esperanza said as he took his turn watching the night light up bright green through night-vision binoculars.

"After what you did to his hand? I doubt it."

Nicholas and Havelock, side by side, armed and ready to conduct an assault, was like being thrown back in time.

When they were SEALs, Havelock was a breacher: an expert with explosives called breaching charges. They were surgical charges that sent most of the blast forward into a room. The breacher's main job was to get the assault team into any place, no matter how difficult it might be. Whether it was utilizing a sledgehammer, a lock-picking set, or explosive charges, the breacher always got the assault team inside the perimeter. Everyone expected Havelock to become a sniper, since he was such an excellent shot. Instead, he decided to become a breacher because, as he succinctly said, "I like to do things up close and personal. And I like to blow shit up."

On the other hand, Esperanza had been a shooter. The nuts and bolts of the Navy SEAL teams, highly skilled in close-quarter battle using a machine pistol, shotgun, 9mm, or revolver. Even a combat knife if called for. Esperanza fired thousands of live rounds as a SEAL. As a cop, he fired only a fraction of that, but certainly many more than most cops ever did during their careers.

"I see something," Esperanza said. "Three o'clock."

A caravan was heading down the deserted street. Two black vans and two SUVs. They were coming to the warehouse to store King's recently purchased drug shipment.

Havelock and Esperanza seriously debated when and where they'd extract King. Problem was, half a dozen heavily armed bodyguards, as well as family members and even children, constantly surrounded the drug dealer. Esperanza didn't want to involve innocent bystanders, so the drop seemed like the best option even though in some ways it was the most difficult and dangerous one.

"Showtime," Esperanza said and they both slipped gas masks over their faces. Esperanza took a deep breath.

All right, Nick. No emotion. Acquire the target and extract.

While the rest of King's crew drove into the warehouse to unload the cargo, two of his men remained behind in one of the SUVs, parked out front and keeping watch.

The warehouse doors had been shut, meaning the men inside the warehouse had no visual as to what was going on outside.

Perfect.

Using mountain-climbers rope, Havelock and Esperanza stealthily rappelled from the roof and landed right behind the SUV. The two men in the front seat were busy keeping an eye on the entrance to the parking lot. Havelock and Esperanza squatted behind the hulking vehicle, Havelock holding the M4 light machine gun with the grenade launcher attached and Esperanza brandishing a Heckler and Koch MP5.

They nodded, and then got on their bellies and crawled to the front of the car. Esperanza took the driver's side and Havelock took the passenger side.

Esperanza popped up first. He shot the driver in the temple, then dropped out of sight as Havelock popped up and shot the other thug in the back of the head.

Esperanza jerked open the door and pulled the driver's corpse out, threw it to the ground, brushed away shattered glass from the seat, and hopped in. There was a walkie-talkie in the other dead thug's hand.

"Everyt'ing clear out there?" a voice asked from the walkie.

Havelock sprinted to the left side of the building entrance, gun aimed forward, while Esperanza put the SUV in reverse, backed up several feet, and then did a U-turn so that he was now facing the entrance. Esperanza put the vehicle in drive, slammed his foot on the accelarator, and zoomed straight toward the entrance. A few feet before impact, Esperanza leapt from the vehicle. He landed on his side and rolled a few times, letting his body go with the force of the momentum. The impact of his shoulder against the asphalt hurt, but it wasn't anything serious. He was instantly on his feet.

As soon as the SUV crashed through the warehouse doors, Havelock stepped forward, launched a tear gas grenade, moved back to his position, and dropped to one knee. Esperanza quickly ran up behind Havelock, stood over him, and aimed his weapon. High and low. They waited. Cool. Collected. Focused. Blind machine gun fire erupted from inside. Esperanza wished he'd worn earplugs, it was so loud.

They didn't return fire. Patiently waited instead.

Three men raced out, their forearms rubbing burning eyes. Tears rolled down their cheeks, and they hacked and shouted and wildly fired their automatics, hoping to get lucky and hit any kind of target.

Havelock and Esperanza fired short, controlled bursts of gunfire. Head and chest. Took out the thugs clean. Bodies dropped in succession like some violent puppet show.

Esperanza needed to be careful and make sure they took King alive. Sweat stung his eyes and he could hear his breathing because of the gas mask. It was slow and steady.

"Don't shoot," a voice yelled from inside the warehouse.

"Come out with your hands over your heads," Esperanza yelled back, voice sounding muffled.

King emerged, flanked by two of his men. Big guys. Their hands were up in the air.

"Don't shoot!" King said again between dry hacks. They all doubled over, attempting to catch their breath. King fell to his knees, bent over, and vomited.

Havelock and Esperanza marched forward. Havelock swept his M4 from side to side and delivered covering fire inside the garage. Esperanza kicked the first thug across the jaw, sending him into a back flip. He smacked the second thug against the back of the head with the butt of the MP5. Then he grabbed King by his dreadlocks and hauled him to his feet.

Got you now, you little prick.

Out of nowhere came the screech of tires. Esperanza jerked his head around to see two Mercedes fly down the street and then make quick, wild turns into the parking lot. One car was silver. One metallic blue. Both sedans. A blond man leaned out the passenger side of the silver Benz and fired what appeared to be an AK-47. King's chest exploded as two bullets cut though him. Esperanza was hit in the chest and stomach, the impact of the slugs knocking him to the ground.

What the fuck is going on?

Havelock dropped to one knee and fired back at the lead vehicle. Hit the front tire. The Benz spun out of control, tires screaming, and the second vehicle barely missed colliding with it. While he continued firing short bursts of gunfire, Havelock grabbed Esperanza by the back of his body armor and hurriedly dragged him into the safety of the warehouse.

"You wounded?" Havelock asked. It was hard to see through the clouds of smoke.

"No," Esperanza said. The vest stopped the bullet, but the pain was still a motherfucker. "Who the fuck are these guys?"

Esperanza leaned over and peeked out. The one advantage he and Havelock had was that the only cover the shooters were able to use was their vehicles, since the parking lot was empty. They all wore expensive designer suits. All were white. All were carrying an impressive amount of firepower.

One of the shooters barked orders at the other men. Sounded like Russian. Esperanza was sure of it. They unloaded a massive barrage of bullets and Esperanza ducked back inside, hot lead ricocheting all over the place.

"There's six of them," Esperanza said. He wanted to remove the gas mask so he could see more clearly. But with all the tear gas hovering in the air, it wasn't even an option.

"Last thing we want is to let them surround us." Havelock slipped a grenade into the M4's launcher. "Let's make a move, while they're still in our sights."

Esperanza slapped a clip into the HK, crouched low, peeked out, aimed his machine pistol, and fired a volley of covering fire. The MP5 spat a fountain of spent shells into the air and over his shoulder, its barrel spewed flames like a metal dragon.

Havelock emerged from behind Esperanza and fired the grenade.

The silver Mercedes exploded into a huge orange and

black fireball. The blast was so powerful the shock wave almost knocked Esperanza to the ground again. One of the Russians shrieked, his body engulfed by flames. His boys gunned him down. Esperanza supposed they wanted to quickly put him out of his misery.

Two down, four to go.

The remaining shooters shouted at each other and immediately hopped into the second Benz, turned the car around, and sped off.

"At least they know how to take a hint," Havelock said.

"Let's get outta here before there are any other surprises."

With his immense hands, Havelock carefully inspected Esperanza's ribs. He poked and prodded and Esperanza winced from the pain. Three big black and blue bruises. Seemed like he'd been the recipient of a major working-over.

"They might be fractured," Havelock said. "Maybe we should head to the hospital and get you some x-rays."

They were in Esperanza's living room. Both smelled of tear gas, cordite, and blood.

"It can wait," Esperanza said as pulled down his T-shirt and sat in the easy chair. There was a bottle of vicodin in the medicine cabinet. He'd pop a couple so he could rest for a little while.

Havelock handed him a crystal snifter filled with brandy and sat on the sofa. "So why did those Russians join the party?"

"Maybe they were coming to rip off King?"

"Possible. We just happened to be in the wrong place at the wrong time."

"Look at the bright side, at least it wasn't the DEA."

"Yeah. We woulda had a lot of *esplainin'* to do."

Esperanza checked his watch. Three a.m. "I wish fuckin' Devona would call."

"Is she playing us?"

"Doubt it. Devona's certainly into theatrics, but this isn't her style. Her vendetta against me is personal." Esperanza was still mentally wired, but his body was at the point of exhaustion. He dropped into the leather recliner and stared at the area where the coffee table used to be, where there was still a urine stain on the expensive Persian rug. "She'd want a much more intimate situation. I'm sure she's getting a kick out of me having to protect her . . . but otherwise, she's got some serious people after her."

"The question is why?"

"Uh-huh. She may or may not know. Since no one, not the Feds, NYPD, or the Justice Department could ever find out anything about her or Rybak's background, we're flying blind here."

"Well, what's the next move?"

"I need to talk to an old acquaintance."

The next morning Esperanza's body was on fire. His ribs. Chest. Shoulder. Hip. A searing carnival of pain was in full swing. The long, hot shower helped a little. So did the three vicodin he took with his coffee.

He was sitting at the breakfast bar in the kitchen, sipping his second cup of Italian espresso and watching the morning news on the fourteen-inch LCD flat screen hanging on the peach-colored wall over the marble counter. The shooting at the warehouse was all over the news. They were calling it a turf war between Jamaican drug dealers and Russian mobsters. The police were happy because they'd recovered over two million dollars in cocaine and marijuana at the warehouse. The DEA was joining the investigation.

The cell phone rang and Esperanza immediately answered it.

"Good morning, Nicholas," Devona said. She sounded quite chipper. "Nice handiwork."

"I guess you watched the news."

"Yeah. Would've preferred to see it in live action, but what's a girl to do?" Esperanza imagined her smiling as she waited for his response. He didn't give her one. "Did you get to interrogate King before you wasted him?"

"Wasn't me. And I didn't get a chance to ask him a goddamned thing before the Russians finished him off."

"Too bad. So, I guess your only lead is the wise guy, Goteri?"

"Looks like it." Esperanza went to the coffee machine and refilled his cup, then added three spoonfuls of sugar. "I need to ask you a couple of questions."

"I'm busy. Let's meet later tonight and we can chat all you want."

"Wait—"

She hung up.

He wondered about Legs. How was she holding up? Was Devona hurting her? Esperanza needed to push those thoughts from his mind. He needed to stay focused and emotionally stolid. His best weapon right now was his mind and his instincts. With Havelock at his side, there was no situation they'd be incapable of handling.

Now he had to find out if an old mobster would be willing to trade in on a twenty-year-old debt and help him get to Goteri. Esperanza wasn't sure what the

Russian mob angle was at the moment, but it didn't matter. Right now he was getting closer to finding out who wanted the head of Mistress Devona Love, and then he'd know the real odds of the game and how much blood he'd have to play for.

Chapter

20

Gino Avallone's three-story brick Colonial Revival–style home was perched on the top of a hill, part of a sprawling piece of land surrounded by elaborate gardens. It had a templelike entrance and multipane, double-hung windows painted white. Simple yet classical styling. Avallone was a man with fine tastes.

Esperanza drove up to the front of the impressive Long Island home and whistled. Being a retired wiseguy obviously had its benefits. He hadn't seen Avallone in many years, yet the former mob boss didn't hesitate to meet with him and invited Esperanza to his home for lunch.

Avallone was one of the last old-school dons during the early nineties. For over two decades the Bureau and the U.S. attorney's office attempted to put Avallone out of business, yet they were never able to hand down a single indictment. His people were extremely loyal. They still believed in the old-fashioned *Omerta*—code of silence. And Avallone was extremely shrewd and never allowed himself to be directly connected to anything remotely criminal. When he saw the power of the New York mob families quickly crumble during the nineties as an end-less stream of RICO indictments were handed down and everyone turned rat, Avallone decided to get out and eventually made the transition to legit dot-com busi-nesses. Internet gambling was generating much more money than the illegal kind. To hell with prostitution: online porn pulled in millions of dollars a year, and you could never be arrested for it.

Esperanza followed Avallone's chubby South American maid in her tight purple pantsuit. Though she was proba-bly close to his mother's age, the maid still had a slam-min' body and Esperanza was certain that good ol' Gino was keeping his afternoons busy with the hired help. They cruised down a long hallway painted regal gold. Hanging on the walls were dozens of framed black-and-white photos of Avallone's swingin' Vegas days of the six-ties. Partying with a slew of celebrities, including the Rat Pack themselves.

The images brought a broad smile to Esperanza's face and he thought about how he came to know Gino Avallone. Esperanza was finishing his last year in Narcotics before switching to Homicide, and his turf was the once wild and decadent streets of Forty-Deuce.

Nicole Avallone was a sixteen-year-old heroin junkie and habitual runaway. And every time Don Avallone or-dered his men to drag her back home, his daughter ran off again. Then she got shacked up with a heroin dealer named Puchi Hernandez. Esperanza was working under-cover as part of Puchi's drug crew. Nicole was probably sleeping with Puchi to spite her father, and Puchi enjoyed bangin' a mafia don's daughter. Nicole was a willowy girl with a sweet disposition, and Esperanza wanted to get her out of such a volatile and potentialy violent environ-ment but couldn't afford to blow his cover. Unfortunately, one night, Nicole overdosed. Puchi was going to let her die, just for the fun of it and because he was bored with her.

"I hate fuckin' junkies," the heroin dealer said as he stood over Nicole and watched her turn blue.

Though it was risky going against his boss, Esperanza gave Nicole mouth-to-mouth and saved her life. Used the excuse that it would be more of a pain to get rid of a dead body than a live one.

Puchi ordered Esperanza to dump Nicole in an alley. Instead, Esperanza took her to his safe house. That almost proved to be a major mistake, since all Nicole wanted to do was go back to her drug dealer boyfriend. Besides that, she wasn't in a rush to quit using junk. Took a lot of persuasion on Esperanza's part, but he finally convinced her that there wasn't much of a future in being a junkie and she went along with it, maybe because she thought the advice was coming from an actual heroin dealer. Esperanza had taken a huge risk. Should've never gotten involved. If he'd blown his cover, Puchi would've put a bullet in his head.

Though it took some time, he helped Nicole get clean and then delivered her back to her father, who was eternally grateful. Fortunately, Nicole finally came to her senses and realized that the lifestyle she was living was only hurting herself and her family, so she went on the straight and narrow after that. Now, Esperanza was smart enough to know that a major mafia don owing you for his little girl's life was a beautiful hand of cards to have. Though he might never need to play that hand, it was well worth having.

Esperanza followed the maid through a cathedral-style doorway and into the living room, which was filled with expensive retro furniture from the 1940s. The floor was covered with cream-colored shag carpeting. Avallone was relaxing in an opulent leather chair and reading the *Wall Street Journal*. He glanced up, grinned, and rushed over to give Esperanza a big affectionate hug, like he was reuniting with his long-lost son.

Standing behind the expansive mahogany bar, Avallone poured Maker's Mark into two ruby-colored bourbon glasses and said, "You look terrific, Nicholas. Barely aged a day in all these years."

"The weekly facials help."

"Sure thirty million didn't hurt too much, either." Esperanza chuckled at that one. "When I read that you won all that moola, *minchia* I so fuckin' happy for you. Talk about somebody who deserved such good fortune." Avallone reached under the bar, produced a humidor with what Esperanza was sure would be top-of-the-line cigars. Got to work on the cigars. "Then that shit that went down last year. How you saved those kids. Some people are natural-born heroes."

"I'm no hero. Just a guy tryin' to do the right thing."

Avallone strolled over with the two glasses of bourbon as well as two Cubans and a gold lighter on a small, antique silver platter. "Whataya think a hero is, my friend?" There were diamond and gold rings on his fingers and a gold watch on his wrist. Avallone moved with the confident grace of a Broadway hoofer. He sported a tropical blue cashmere V-neck sweater and brown corduroy pants. At sixty-eight, he was the picture of perfect health. Tanned skin and a full head of silver hair combed back.

"How's Nicole?" Esperanza asked as Avallone lit his cigar for him. Yes, a man of fine tastes.

"She's doin' great. Married, kids." Esperanza noticed besides the smell of cigar smoke, the room was filled with the scent of a couple of dozen freshly cut roses, which were placed in crystal vases that sparkled with the bright afternoon sunlight streaming in though the majestic double windows. "Whole nine yards. God bless." Avallone smiled. It was an ingratiating, generous smile. One that belonged to a proud father and grandfather.

Avallone sat down in an open arm club chair with a polished walnut frame and sun gold velvet upholstery.

"Good for her."

He sipped the Maker's Mark and gazed at Esperanza, his big brown eyes gleaming with warmth under bushy silver eyebrows. Then his expression turned serious. Very businesslike. "Why you need a meet with a scumbag like Goteri?"

"I take it you're not a fan?"

"Organized crime ain't as organized as it used to be," Avallone said with a sad wag of his head. "A jerk-off like Goteri's a capo? Total fuckin' cowboy. Degenerate gambler. Got John Gotti aspirations. But none of the brains. None of the style. None of the charm. In the old days, he woulda been a *babbo*. A low-level underling. A wannabe. Nothin' else."

"Got a lot of guns?"

"If he needs 'em . . . yeah. You planning on takin' him down?"

"Just wanna have a nice civil chat with him."

"And you want me to set it up?"

"Yeah. But if this meet goes south . . . would this be a problem for you?"

"Nah," Avallone said with a dismissive wave of the hand. "If something was to happen to Goteri, there are ten young Turks ready to take his place, and they got no sense of loyalty. *La Cosa Nostra* . . . it's practically a pile of fuckin' ashes. Ancient history. Fodder for TV shows."

Avallone closed his eyes for a moment and sniffed his bourbon, enjoying the aroma. Took a sip. "Funny, when the five *famiglias* fell apart under the RICO prosecution of the eighties and nineties? The mafia was *finito* and it was supposeta be better for the city? Yeah, right. We got replaced by the crazy fuckin' Colombians. The Jamaicans. Chinese Triads. And the worst of worst, the Red Mafiya."

"The Russians. Can you tell me about them?"

"Sure. Top of the line. They're an international organization. As you probably know, a lot of members are ex-KGB. Ex-military. They're involved in every-fuckin'-thing. From billions of dollars in money laundering to smugglin' African diamonds. Got their greedy fingers in tropical casinos, prostitution, you name it. Can't go to Brighton Beach and spit without hitting a member of the Red Mafiya. And they ain't got no rules like us. They'll do a hit on a cop, a prosecutor, an FBI agent. Ruthless as they come, my friend."

"Goteri have any connections to them?"

"I hear he's tryin' to get in bed with them. Lookin' for new business opportunities. Little Italy's a thing of the past. Besonhurst, Bay Ridge . . . got more Chinks than Wops these days. "

King.
Russians.
Goteri.
Russians.

Not too hard to figure out who was out to bump off the mistress; the trick was narrowing it down to a specific mobster. Next trick would be taking them out. Wasn't going to be easy. Could Goteri be behind this for some reason, or was the Russian mob involvement just coincidence?

"Ever hear of Goteri connected to human trafficking?"

"Nah. I don't think that even Goteri would sink that fuckin' low. Why?"

"Nothing." Esperanza finished off his bourbon. "I appreciate your help with this."

"You know, every time I play with my granddaughter, Frannie? I think about what you did for Nicole." Avallone sighed. Grinned. "Anytime you need anything, Nick, you know you can come to me."

"Thanks, Gino."

"I'll make some calls and let ya know what I come up with." Avallone rose to his feet and took the empty glass from Esperanza. "C'mon. I got a real nice lunch set up for us."

Chapter
21

O'Leary's Bar in the Village was an Irish joint stuck in time. Genuine throwback to the 1960s. The kind of dive that prided itself on dim and dank. Sawdust on the floor. Dark paneled walls. No kamikazes or apple martinis or cosmopolitans. Beer. Lager. Scotch. Whisky. Bourbon.

There were a couple of ancient alkies discussing soccer with the white-haired bartender who kept shouting, "Fook that!" while drying shot glasses with a stained rag.

Lounging in some of the wide oak booths with torn green vinyl padding were groups of artsy kids from NYU getting smashed on hard liquor. Elvis Costello was crooning "Alison" from the juke.

Havelock and Esperanza were drinking shots of Jameson and pints of Bass Ale.

Esperanza rubbed his side and felt a slight shot of pain. Fractured rib, probably. Baby stuff.

"How do you wanna deal with the Eye-talians?" Havelock asked.

"I want to avoid a shootout, for once," Esperanza said. "Devona and I will go in. Stay outside, locked and loaded. Anything remotely funny seems to go down, come in. Shoot first. Ask questions later."

"Don't you think it's a bad idea takin' *la loca* in there?"

"She's not giving me a choice."

As if on cue, Devona pranced into O'Leary's. Everyone in the joint stopped talking. Stopped drinking. Stopped breathing, for that matter, as all eyes locked on Devona like heat-seeking missiles as she floated across the room. Black latex coat. Swirl of hair held up by silver Chinese hair sticks. Big Chanel sunglasses. Leather gloves. Thousand-dollar designer handbag. Esperanza swore he heard Wagner's "Ride of the Valkyries" playing in his head. Perfect theme for the Mistress.

She stopped at their booth, placed her hands on her hips, and grinned devilishly.

"Hello, boys." She held out her hand. "You must be Havelock."

"The infamous Mistress Love."

Havelock stood up, took her hand, and shook it. Devona held it as her eyes marched up and down the big man's impressive physique. Havelock was checking her out as well, but for different reasons. Esperanza guessed he wanted to size up the woman who'd wreaked havoc on his friend's life. Devona seductively caressed Havelock's broad, muscular chest.

"My, my. You're a lot of man, aren't you?" She sounded all giddy. "I could definitely have some fun with you."

"I might be too much to handle, baby," Havelock said, letting her touch him. He appeared to be enjoying the lustful attention. "Even for you."

"Enough with the pleasantries," Esperanza said. Everything had to be a game with Devona.

Devona slipped in on Havelock's side of the booth and

Havelock sat beside her. She snuggled up close to him. As much as Havelock kept his cool, Esperanza could see in his eyes that he wasn't immune to Mistress Love's charms. Seemed like nobody was.

"Have you ever been involved with The Red Mafiya?" Esperanza was rolling the dice on this. He wanted to see if she was going to completely lie, or give him some kind of genuine info. Or some kind of reaction that might tell him something. Anything.

"Russians? Why do you ask?"

"Because, as you well know, they showed up and killed King and tried to kill us. And they seem to be the connecting factor."

She thought about it for a moment, her index finger tapping her chin, then her face lit up. "Oleksei! That's the only one I know of. Never met him personally, though. Have no idea why he'd want me dead."

"How do you know him?"

"He had business dealings with Bishop."

"What kind of business dealings?"

"Bishop helped him smuggle young ladies from Serbia, Croatia, and Russia, to work in his brothels and for his escort services." Esperanza thought of Alina, and it angered him that Devona was telling them about this as if she was talking about shipping livestock. An everyday occurrence. "Some ended up in the States, others were shipped to Yakuza in Japan. Japanese businessmen love young, pale blondes. Some ended up in the Middle East."

"And what was your connection to this?"

"Jason and I sometimes played intermediaries." She shrugged, obviously not willing to commit to anything. "It was a very complicated arrangement and I didn't pay attention to the details."

"You ever do anything to piss Oleksei off?"

"Not that I know of. Like I said, never even met the man."

"Fine. Now, when we go to see Goteri, let's keep things civil. Let me ask the questions."

"Sure. You're the boss."

Chapter

22

The Genaro Social Club was located in a storefront on Eighteeth Avenue in Bensonhurst, Brooklyn. The one-story brick building was sandwiched between a Chinese restaurant and a pharmacy. The sign hanging on the front was so old it was fading and almost unreadable. Ghosts of the past. Twenty years ago, there'd be wiseguys standing outside smoking cigars, drinking beer, and laughing it up. Though times had changed, the residential area still had a strong Italian flavor. On the avenue there was an Italian bakery, a pizzeria, and a pasta joint. Of course, there was also a Starbucks on the corner.

It was late at night, so the street was nearly deserted. They were parked right across the street. Esperanza looked over at the social club. Venetian blinds covered the windows and the door was painted black.

Esperanza pulled his Sig from his hip holster and slipped it in the glove compartment.

"If you're carrying a weapon, Devona, give it up."

"Why would I need a weapon when I got you?"

"Oh, this is going to be fun."

* * *

They strolled into the social club, Devona's arm casually hooked around Esperanza's. Immediately assessing the environment, Esperanza swept his eyes across the dimly lit room. There were a bunch of circular tables, a lengthy oak bar that needed a good polishing, and an old-fashioned brass espresso machine. The place smelled of bitter coffee and cigarettes and sweet anisette. An ancient jukebox played Led Zeppelin's "Stairway to Heaven." Unexpected theme music for mobsters.

There were two men in charcoal gray double-breasted suits. One was fat, around six feet tall. Crew cut. The other was shorter and had so much muscle, it seemed like his suit jacket was going to burst at the seams. Curly hair and lots of flashy gold jewelry.

Hands dangled at their sides. Fingers firmly gripped 9mm Berettas.

At the far end of the room, sitting at a table under a scoop light, a lazy swirl of smoke floating over his head, was Richie Goteri, sucking on a cigarette and sipping from a small espresso cup. He was pretty much how Gino described him: receding black hair with a widow's peak right above his prominent forehead. Jagged scar on his cheek. Beady eyes. Broad, pockmarked nose. Feeble chin. Thin mustache. Spanking-new black leather jacket over a bright red turtleneck.

"Frankie's gonna frisk ya while Rico keeps an eye on ya," Goteri said.

"Fine."

The fat mobster stepped forward and Esperanza held his arms up and out.

"Who's the broad?" Goteri asked.

"Devona Love," Esperanza said. In an instant, guns were aimed at Esperanza and Devona. "Whoa, fellas. You need to chill."

"*Minquia*. You got some balls bringin' her here," Goteri said and stubbed out his cigarette. "Why shouldn't I clip the both of ya right now?"

Frankie patted Esperanza down while Rico kept his gun trained on Devona.

"Well, for one, my brother, who's a federal agent, knows I'm here. So the organized crime unit would be all up in your business," Esperanza said and then smirked. He was lying, of course, since Mark didn't know a damn thing. "Two, parked across the street inside the Escalade is my backup. Big guy. Ex Navy SEAL. Has an HK MP5 submachine gun on his lap. Thirty-round mag."

Goteri jutted his chin toward the window. Rico, who kept his gun pointed at Devona, stepped to the window and peered through the dusty blinds.

"Shooting starts and he'll storm through that door," Esperanza continued. "And trust me, these two mooks won't stand a chance. So if Devona and I die, everybody dies."

"Yeah, there's a big fuckin' *moolie* parked across the street," Rico said. "He's lookin' over here. Just smiled. Moolie's got a machine pistol pointed this way." He turned and looked at Goteri. "Whataya want me to do, boss?"

"Frisk the broad," Goteri said.

Frankie took his sweet time frisking Devona, grubby hands exploring every curve and crevice.

"I hope this doesn't mean we're engaged or anything," she said.

"Shuddup," he said. "Let me see them hair pins." She took out the first one. The tip was rounded, so it posed no danger. Same with the other one. Frankie then searched through her purse and handed it back to her, looked back at Goteri, and nodded, letting him know that Devona and Esperanza were clean.

"OK, Esperanza," Goteri said. "You got ten minutes."

Devona and Esperanza sauntered over to the table. Devona slipped out of her coat. She wore a rubber mini dress with matching thigh-high boots. The outfit was fire engine red and was decorated with dozens of zippers in very provocative places. The revealing dress highlighted Devona's ample cleavage.

Goteri gave her a head-to-toe once-over but didn't seem too impressed by Devona's womanly assets.

Esperanza sat in the chair opposite Goteri, while Devona took a seat on the mobster's left side. She rested her chin in her hand and stared him down.

" 'Smatter," Devona said. "You don't like girls?"

"I'm just tryin' to figure out what the big fuss is all about. You don't look so dangerous to me."

"Yeah. It's all rumors. I'm practically a nun." She glanced at Esperanza, who scowled, not appreciating her little inside joke. "I guess that's why that hitter you sent . . . What was his name? Cole Blue. That's why he's swimmin' wit da fishies, as you wise guys say."

Goteri sipped his espresso and his eyelid twitched and cheeks turned red. "You should show some fuckin' respect."

"Look," Esperanza said. He needed to keep things civil. Probably impossible with Mistress Love in the room. "We want to know who gave you the order to put a hit on Devona."

"Nobody gives me fuckin' orders. It was a business favor."

"Tell us who it was and we'll be on our merry way," Esperanza said.

"You believe this fuckin' spic?" Goteri said to his men. The vein on his temple was pulsating. "Got some fuckin' nerve. Waltzes in here with this *putana*, who likes mouthin' off, and he starts makin' demands." Goteri mashed his cigarette in the plastic ashtray. "I don't give a shit who you know. Avallone? Fuck 'im. You're an ex-cop? Fuck you."

Devona giddily clapped her hands three times and grinned. "Wow . . . this is wonderful. With all the macho goombah dialogue, I feel like I'm in a Martin Scorsese flick."

"You're awfully chippy for a broad who's got a price on her head."

Devona leaned forward, and this time, Goteri scoped out her cleavage. Her breasts seemed as if they were going to pop out of her mini dress and Esperanza could see Goteri's mouth was watering.

"I like to look at life on the positive side." She took out a silver oval-shaped compact from her handbag, flicked it open, checked her make-up, closed it, and left it on the table.

"You're a nice piece of ass," Goteri said. "Too bad you ain't gonna be around long."

"Ever had your palm read?"

"No."

"May I?"

"Why should I let you?"

"Grant a poor girl her last wish?"

Esperanza wasn't sure what Devona was up to. It made him nervous. Frankie was suddenly standing close, gun barrel a couple of inches from Esperanza's temple.

Behave yourself, Devona. Don't get us killed.

Goteri chuckled and shook his head. "You are one crazy fuckin' bitch." He held out his hand. "Here. Knock yourself out."

She slid her chair close, grabbed his hand and played with his fingers, then caressed his palm. Goteri smirked, amused by Devona's audacity. "You have a long life line. Oooh . . . very virile. A man who knows how to please a woman."

Goteri laughed. "Tell me something I don't know."

"You're way overconfident."

Devona was incredibly fast. She pulled the first hairpin, pressed the top, and the rounded plastic point ejected, revealing the point of a sharp metal blade. She stabbed Goteri's palm and pinned his hand to the table. Goteri yelped. She did the same move with the second hairpin and jammed that one against his neck. Her flowing hair fell to her shoulders in what seemed like slow motion.

Esperanza sprang into action. His hand came up in a quick arc, hooked around Frankie's gun hand, twisted, and he simultaneously did a leg sweep, and the arch of his foot nailed Frankie right behind the knee. Esperanza snatched the gun from the wiseguy, reeled around, and aimed it at Rico as Frankie landed on his back and the room shook. Esperanza thrust the heel of his boot against Frankie's throat. Rico aimed his gun at Esperanza but his eyes were filled with uncertainty.

"Put the gun down or I'll cut his carotid artery and blood will gush like a fountain," Devona said. "Take only a few seconds for him to bleed out."

"Better do as she says." Esperanza pressed his foot down harder and Frankie gagged. "Besides, I'm a damn fine shot."

Goteri stared into Devona's eyes and he gulped. She gave the hairpin a slight twist and a trickle of blood snaked down his neck.

"Drop it, Rico," the capo ordered.

Rico reluctantly lowered his hand, uncocked his weapon, and let it fall to the tile floor. Esperanza pulled his boot from Frankie's throat. Fat Boy was turning blue.

He clutched his throat, wheezed, and rolled over. Esperanza got up and retrieved Rico's gun. He winked at Rico and then pistol-whipped him. Rico fell to his knees, blood trickling from the cut over his eyebrow.

"That's for calling my friend an eggplant, you racist fuck."

While Esperanza kept a watchful eye on the bodyguards, Devona turned around and gave her full attention to Goteri.

"Okay, Goteri. Are you going to tell me what I want to know? Or are you willing to learn that everything about my reputation is not only true, but actually much worse?"

She pulled the hairpin about an inch away from Goteri's neck.

"Go fuck yourself," Goteri said, remaining defiant.

Oh, boy. Fool doesn't understand who he's dealing with.

Devona stuck the hairpin between Goteri's legs and he screamed. His eyes got so wide, they seemed like they might pop out of their sockets.

"I'm going to put this pin through your little prick so many times, it'll be ground beef by the time I'm done."

"Okay. Christ." Goteri was stammering now. Not so tough anymore. "His name is Dragoslav."

"Mato Dragoslav?"

"Yeah. He's a Russian gangster."

"Dragoslav's no gangster. Not Russian, either. He's a Serb. But he works for the Russians."

"Said his boss was looking for you. Wanted you dead. If I gave them a hand, they were gonna help me expand my business. Neighborhood's changed. Lotta Russians livin' here now."

"Why would they need a weasel like you? Russian mafiya make you wise guys look like clowns."

"I got no fuckin' idea. I swear."

"Why was King in on this?"

"My men couldn't find you, so Dragoslav put a bounty on your head. Two hundred large. Everybody on the street's huntin' for you."

"Nice." Devona nodded. Seemed like she was impressed she was worth so much dead. "You know why?"

"Got no idea." Devona twisted her fist and Goteri yelped. All the men in the room held their breath, including Esperanza. "Please, I swear, that's all I know."

"I believe you. Now let me give you a piece of advice." She brought the tip of the pin to his right nostril. "Keep your mouth shut. You think I'm dangerous? Esperanza over there, he's someone you don't wanna fuck with. Trust me, Slick. So we're gonna walk out of here and you're gonna forget you ever saw us."

Goteri blinked. Too scared to move. A sharp blade to the penis will do that to a guy.

Devona tossed the hairpin to the floor, stood up, and put on her coat. "*Vamonos, muchacho,*" she said in perfect Spanish and strutted past Esperanza, who was still holding the guns on the thugs. "Nice chatting with you boys."

Devona and Esperanza hurriedly crossed the street and climbed into the Escalade. Havelock had the motor running and the machine pistol on his lap.

"Everything go okay?" Havelock asked.

"You could say that," Esperanza said.

"I suggest you drive away," Devona said. "Now."

Havelock put the SUV in gear and pulled out.

"Why the big rush?" Esperanza turned around and stared at her, wondering what she was up to.

"I left my purse behind." She smirked.

Boom. There was an explosion. The windows from the social club shattered, spewing black plumes of smoke.

The intense force of the blast shook the SUV and they all jerked forward. Havelock stepped on the gas.

"Are you fuckin' nuts?" Esperanza said.

"Woo hoo!" Devona threw her head back and let out a crazy laugh. "Are we having fun or what?" She bent forward, sticking her head between Havelock and Esperanza. "Come on, Nick. You think Goteri wouldn't have sent people after you? Or been on the phone letting Dragoslav know we came to see him?"

"How the hell did you learn to rig an explosive like that?" Havelock asked.

"Jason had a military background just like you two. There's a lot he taught me. The compact was the timer. Detonator and plastic explosive was tucked in the lining of the purse." She patted Esperanza on the shoulder. "So remember, Nicholas. Never underestimate me."

"I hear that," Havelock said, and though he seemed to fight it, he still grinned. "Damn. You are one bad bitch."

Havelock got on the Belt Parkway. Slowed down a little. "Who is this Dragoslav?"

"A courier. Worked for Oleksei and Bishop."

"So it all comes back to Oleksei. Are you sure you're telling me everything?"

She held up her hand. There was smear of Goteri's blood on her palm. "Scout's honor, babe."

Chapter

23

The license plate was registered under the name Sheila McMurphy. Connecticut. Sixty years old. Deceased. That lead was a dead end for Santos. But the credit card? It gave him an actual address. Under an alias, of course. Mary Yanovic. Santos figured it was another stolen identity. The driver's license appeared on the computer monitor. Sure wasn't Devona. Some fat broad with bad skin and even worse hair.

Crafty chica. Who is she, really?

Gnawing on a pencil, Santos wondered if he should call Esperanza and tell him he might have found some kind of actual trail to Devona. No. He'd wait to find out if this was a solid lead or just another dead end. Check it out first, and then let Esperanza know.

The other night, it had thrown Santos for a loop when he was staking out Esperanza's building and Esperanza's car pulled up down the block and Esperanza and Devona climbed out, then hopped in a cab. Though Santos was stunned, he immediately followed the cab. He'd confront Esperanza later. At first, Santos thought, maybe

Esperanza fell under the domina's spell and he was bangin' her? The idea was crazy.

Then it all became very clear: *Legs is missing.* He knew that. He checked. Nobody had seen her in the last couple of days. Devona must have kidnapped her and was forcing Esperanza to work for her. That was the only logical explanation. *But why?* Why would the Black Widow need Esperanza's help? Maybe it was one of her elaborate psychological games, some off-the-wall revenge scheme. Santos wished Esperanza had confided in him. But then again, he understood why. Good ol' Santos, always does everything by the book. Never breaks the rules.

He rubbed his tired, burning eyes. The precinct house was relatively empty since it was nearly four a.m. Santos's stomach grumbled. He grabbed a wilted French fry from the Styrofoam container, stuffed it in his mouth, and slowly chewed it. It was cold and tasted like crap, but beat a blank. The office chair squeaked as Santos leaned forward and read the address off the dusty monitor screen and scribbled it on a yellow Post-it note.

That night, he'd managed to shadow Devona's taxi without her spotting him. She got out at a parking garage on the Upper East Side, went in, and drove off in a Benz. Nice sedan.

A few blocks later, she stopped off at a twenty-four-hour pharmacy. Santos continued to tail her. Unfortunately, there wasn't much traffic, so he needed to keep his distance, and eventually he lost sight of her. He returned to the pharmacy. Flashed his gold shield. Cashier said Devona had used a credit card. Volunteered a copy of the receipt.

Now he was close. Had an address. A building in Tribeca. Didn't mean that's where she was actually hiding out. Where she might be holding Legs captive.

But he'd soon find out.

* * *

"Why do you want to cuff me?" Legs asked. She was sitting on the cot. She was glad Otto gave her a clean sweatshirt and sweatpants.

"Just do what I say," Devona said, handcuffs dangling from her index finger. "Stand up and turn around." Legs turned around and Devona cuffed her. At least they weren't too tight. "Sit." Like a good slave, Legs obeyed.

Reclining in a metal folding chair, Devona was dressed casual for once. Tight, straight-leg blue jeans, cowboy boots, and a cream-colored pullover sweater. With that outfit, Legs figured she didn't have anything bad planned. Devona obviously liked to dress for the occasion.

Otto entered the cage. In one hand, he carried a tray with a silk napkin draped over it, and in the other hand, he had a folding TV table. He set the TV table in front of Legs, gently placed the tray on it, and pulled away the silk napkin.

Teriyaki-glazed salmon. Asparagus in garlic cream. Arugula with walnuts and balsamic vinaigrette. A glass of white wine. The scrumptious aroma of the gourmet meal made Legs salivate and her stomach churn.

"Hungry?"

"No."

"Don't be stupid, Legs."

Why fight it? This was the way Devona wanted to do things; Legs should just go along with her wishes. Hell. She could be feeding Legs bread and water, so a real meal was much more appetizing.

"Okay. Yes, I'm hungry."

"Good. I'm going to feed you."

Otto left. So quiet, Legs hadn't even noticed.

"I can feed myself."

"Not with those handcuffs on," Devona said with a sly

smile as she cut a piece of fish. She stabbed it with the fork and held it up to Legs's nose. Legs closed her eyes, took in the delectable aroma, and her mouth opened. Devona dropped the piece in. Legs slowly chewed and savored the taste. The hint of flavorful sake. Sweet mirin rice wine. Slightly sour soy sauce. Devona smiled even more broadly. She appeared awfully happy to be feeding Legs.

"Like it?"

"Yes."

"I'm glad. Cooked it just for you." She continued to feed Legs. Didn't rush her. Let her enjoy the fine meal. There was something very sensual about the interaction. "Nicholas is getting closer. Your time here might end soon."

"You're really going to keep your word?"

"Yes, Legs. I am." She picked up the wineglass, brought it to Legs's lips, tilted the glass, and Legs sipped it. Italian. Good vintage. Not too dry. "Do you want to know where your boyfriend and I are going tonight?"

Legs's stomach twisted. "No. Not really."

"Such a terrible liar." Devona lovingly dabbed Legs's mouth with a paper napkin. "Nick and I are going to an erotic couples party. Those parties can get quite . . . dirty."

"I thought you're trying to find out who wants to kill you." Legs knew Devona was egging her on, and the worst part was, it was working. "What does a swing party have to do with that?"

"Don't be jealous. There's a reason we're going there. To see a contact of mine named Nataya. She might be able to help us find the person we're looking for. It's for business reasons." Devona's eyes seemed to catch fire. Whatever she was thinking, it seemed to make her all hot and bothered. "Doesn't mean we can't have a little fun while we're there. Hey, you know Nicholas, he's got that wild streak. So anything's possible."

Legs wanted to tell Devona how pathetic she was, using cheap theatrics like that simply to piss her off. To make her *celosa*. Instead, she said, "Nicholas is his own man."

But could she trust Esperanza? She always had, but now? She wasn't so sure. Did she doubt her love for him, too? No. Never doubt that, no matter what. *He'd give his life for you in a second, don't you ever forget that.* Legs realized that Devona was playing her exactly the way she wanted to.

"So you won't mind if I grab a group of girls and we have a party with him?"

Legs wanted to lunge forward and sink her teeth in Devona's throat. Drink her blood. She meekly lowered her head.

"It's your world, Mistress."

"Yes, it is. And don't you ever forget it."

Chapter
24

Devona gave Esperanza the 411. Nataya was Dragoslav's ex-wife. Young and drop-dead gorgeous. You'd think she was the one who walked out on the pug-ugly, middle-aged man. Not the case. When Nataya turned thirty, Dragoslav thought she was over the hill. Literally kicked her to the curb and shacked up with a nineteen-year-old. Nataya worked at an escort service for a while but then decided to make money for herself. She decided to start a "sensualist movement" and put together swing parties for the young, attractive, and rich. In a couple of years, her parties blossomed into legendary feasts of the flesh. Famous actors, singers, and sports figures attended the exclusive events. Nataya was now living large.

Devona and Ryback attended Nataya's parties several times, and though Devona missed the sadomasochistic flavor, she liked the generous sensuality of the soirées. No man was allowed to touch Devona, though. She usually got into a romp with a group of hot women while Ryback and other boyfriends and husbands eagerly watched the female orgy and prayed in vain that they'd be invited to join in.

Standing in the foyer entrance to a huge loft, Devona and Esperanza wore nothing but white terry-cloth towels.

"This is a hell of a way to conduct an interview," Esperanza said.

"Remember. We're undercover. You're my lover, so act like it."

"Why couldn't you just call her on the phone and ask her about Dragoslav?"

"What if she knows about the bounty and sets us up? This way, we surprise her."

"Nothing's easy with you."

"Why don't you relax?" She adjusted her towel since her breasts were about to spill out. "You just might enjoy yourself."

Through sheer curtains, Esperanza could see into the loft. There were Japanese shoji screen room dividers made of black lacquer frames and featuring lovely paintings of geishas and landscapes. Behind the shades, rising and falling shadows revealed a variety of erotic couplings. Soft candlelight and soothing strawberry incense set the mood. Flowing silk banners of gold dangled from the ceilings. Plush red silk pillows lay everywhere. A chorus of moans underscored soft sitar music. Naked couples cruised around holding hands. Some carried crystal flutes filled with bubbly while others sampled coconut shrimp, crab croquettes, and chocolate-covered strawberries being served by waitresses wearing only frilly aprons and stiletto heels.

A naked woman with spectacular breasts, a slim, muscular body, and curly orange tresses strolled over to Esperanza and Devona. She was all smiles and sparkling emerald eyes.

"Hi, I'm Vanessa," she said in a slight Russian accent.

"You must remove the towels if you are going to join the party." Her attention stayed on Devona, not Esperanza. Devona smirked; her eyes locked with Vanessa's as she whipped off her towel with a flourish and handed it over. When Vanessa grabbed the towel, Devona jerked her forward and tongue kissed her. Vanessa immediately surrendered. By the way she pressed her body against Devona's, Esperanza could see Vanessa was in heaven. While kissing Vanessa, Devona reached back and yanked Esperanza's towel loose and let it drop to the floor. Then she grabbed his wrist, drew him against her, and rubbed her lovely, heart-shaped ass against Esperanza's crotch while she continued making out with Vanessa. Esperanza tried to fight it but it was an exercise in futility. He got hard in a matter of seconds.

Do you have any kind of self-control, Nicholas? Or are you a slave to your dick? No. It's an involuntary reaction. Yeah, that's a good one. Involuntary.

Devona suddenly shoved Vanessa away, almost knocking her off her feet. Vanessa grinned, face shiny with saliva. She picked up the towels, threw Devona a kiss, and sashayed away, flawless little butt swaying from side to side.

Devona reeled around, and in one smooth motion, slipped Esperanza's stiff *bicho* between her thighs and pressed her bosom against his chest, nipples erect and her breasts smooth and warm and heaving. She didn't put him inside her. Instead, she squeezed her muscular thighs so tight that it hurt. Hurt so good. Devona leisurely pumped her hips back and forth; there was a raging fire between those amazing thighs and her hot juices dripped all over Esperanza's cock. Her eyes searched his. Her expression was pure predator.

"Wouldn't you love to fuck me right now?" She licked

his neck and then backed away, grabbed his erection, and led him into the party.

On a plush velvet ottoman, in the middle of one of the larger partitioned areas, Esperanza sat beside Devona. They were surrounded by dozens of men and women awash in soft golden light, screwing their brains out. Esperanza tried to look away from the erotic revelry. Couldn't. Threesomes. Foursomes. Moresomes. Lovely bodies. Fit bodies. Mostly vanilla, but some cinnamon and chocolate thrown into the mix. While Esperanza was in the middle of a live porn flick, Legs was locked in some cage, in some dank basement somewhere. He closed his eyes. He should just walk away and not play this game with Devona. But he knew that would be a mistake.

Where was Havelock now? Easy to be stoic during a gunfight, but under this set of circumstances? A different story. When the Mistress was in control? It was her domain, and emotions were meant to run amok.

From the expensive speaker system, a hypnotic industrial beat thumped. Esperanza recognized the song. "#1 Crush" by the band Garbage. The lead singer's haunting voice quivered with frantic desire:

I would burn for you,
Feel pain for you . . .

Would Devona make him have sex with her? He might go berserk and strangle her to death. Or he might simply lose himself in her sumptuous decadence and he'd have every excuse in the world as to why he *had* to do it.

I would crawl on hands and knees
Until you see,
You're just like me . . .

The smell of sweat, musk, cologne, perfume, and most of all, pussy, was intoxicating.

The sounds of ass slapping. The pleading moans. The screams of delight. The sounds of sucking and slurping. The sexy music. All of it made Esperanza's mind spin out of control. He thought he was going to jump out of his skin.

Earlier in the evening, Devona had asked around for Nataya. They said she was expected to arrive in about half an hour. Esperanza could tell Devona was happy about the wait. It would give her the opportunity to mess with his head. To lead him down the path of debauchery he was all too familiar with.

Then she'll go back and tell Legs every detail.

Devona was watching the carnal festivities and fervently fingering herself. Mistress Love made masturbation an art form. Esperanza sat there, all stiff, in more ways than one. A couple of handsome men tried to convince Devona to join them. She shook her head and they respectfully slinked away, back to whomever they were banging.

Then this fine Asian babe came crawling on hands and knees through the knot of undulating bodies. Slender figure and waist-length, pistachio red hair. Nipples pierced with silver rings. An elaborate tattoo of a dragon slithered from her ankle up to her shoulder. She kneeled in front of Devona, her onyx eyes turning feral while they drank in the image of the Mistress fingering herself.

"My name is Lana," she said. "I want to eat your pussy." Then she patiently waited for an invitation.

At first, it seemed like some kind of sexual stand-off since Devona ignored Lana for a very long time. Then she reached out, placed the palm of her hand against the back of Lana's head, and crammed the eager *chinita's* face between her thighs. Lana adeptly lapped and licked and Devona groaned in delight. Mistress leaned her head on

Esperanza's shoulder and moaned in his ear. Lana stared up at Esperanza with seductive eyes while she voraciously serviced Devona with her tongue and lips. The image was simply . . . beautiful.

He was so overwhelmed by a chaotic jumble of emotions—desire, rage, and excitement—it made him want to scream.

"God, she eats pussy soooo good," Devona whispered. "But not as good as Legs does."

His hands balled into fists and he was about to bolt when Devona hooked her arm around his waist, her grip tight. He wasn't going anywhere. "Don't you dare fucking move or there'll be consequences. What? It upsets you that your girlfriend and I partied? That she's no saint, either?" She bucked her hips, slamming her pussy hard against Lana's face, which was glimmering with Devona's juices. "Didn't take a lot of convincing. I didn't force her. Remember, she had a big crush on Sister Terez, which meant she had a big crush on *moi*." Between moans and squeals, Devona continued to taunt him. "So I let her explore that side of herself and she made me come more times than you can imagine. It was soft and sensual and wild and tender." She reached down with her free hand and stroked his erection. Nimble fingers went to work, blood raged, arousal possessed him, and he jerked his hips to the rhythm of Devona's expert hand job. Lana decided to join the festivities, so she reached over and fondled Esperanza's balls, her touch enticing and graceful and flush with experience. Esperanza opened his legs a little wider, offering them both more room to play. Devona continued, "Legs and I. Two best girls losing themselves in each other's touch. Ah, heaven."

Esperanza knew it was all lies. Or was it? Anything was possible. Look where he was at the moment.

What if Devona and Legs got down and dirty? He didn't have the right to be angry. He was doing the same, wasn't he? So how could he possibly complain? Was Legs seduced by Devona? What a surprise. Now Legs would understand. Now she'd believe.

Esperanza closed his eyes and each breath came quicker than the last as he surrendered to all those lovely fingers. Devona's nails dug into his flesh and her hand jerked him faster and faster as her hips rose in the air and her thighs clamped around Lana's head. A scream of delight emerged from deep inside Devona and every muscle in her body tensed as she climaxed. It was electric. Esperanza was swept away by the power of Devona's spectacular orgasm, and he began to moan, his body a slave to her and Lana's talented hands.

Devona's body became slack and her breathing slowed while her hand stroked and tugged and squeezed his *bicho*, and over and over, she passionately whispered in his ear.

"Oh, Legs. Oh, Legs . . ."

Then Esperanza trembled and growled and came between Lana's perfect breasts, and rubbed the tip of his cock against soft, warm flesh, and lost himself in a flutter of kisses, and for a moment, nothing else mattered, except floating on waves of sheer bliss.

Nataya finally arrived. When she saw Devona, she seemed both startled and genuinely delighted to reunite with her old friend. Esperanza didn't like the fact that Nataya looked *that* surprised. Made him a bit suspicious. But Devona was taking the lead on this, so he hoped she also noticed.

After a brief conversation between old friends, Devona and Esperanza were invited to Nataya's private "play" area. The floor was covered with large silk pillows. Vases were filled with lovely white roses. And the ceiling was covered with satin drapes.

In all her naked glory, Nataya was lying on her side on a pillow while she held a flute of champagne. Esperanza admired her exquisite, voluptuous body. Wide hips, thick thighs, full breasts. She had a broad face and sharp cheekbones. Her wide-set bedroom eyes were hypnotic, the color of a turquoise ocean. This was the woman Dragoslav had unceremoniously kicked to the curb because she was too old? Esperanza figured he must be a piece of work.

"Why do you want to know where to find that pig Dragoslav?" Nataya flicked back the golden waves of hair that came down to her freckled shoulders.

"Better you don't know." Devona was sitting between Esperanza's legs, her head against his chest. His forearm loosely rested across her neck. "Better you don't say you ever saw me."

"Are you in some kind of trouble?"

"Don't ask any questions, love."

"You're the Mistress." She took a sip of champagne. "I think I have an address for him."

"What can you tell us about Oleksei?"

The blood seemed to drain from her face and she stiffened.

"I prefer not to say anything, except that he is a very powerful and very dangerous man." There was a nervous tremor in her voice. She gulped down the rest of the champagne. "If he signs your death sentence, not even God can save you."

"Well, we must be going." Devona's fingers crawled up and down Esperanza's thighs.

Nataya pouted and then said, "Oh no, stay and play for

little while. It has been so long." Those wide eyes stared at Esperanza with pure lust. He was an object she wanted to possess. She sure didn't appear nervous anymore. "And I'd like to get a crack at this handsome new slave of yours."

Esperanza couldn't see Devona's expression and waited to hear her answer.

Devona leaned to the side, turned around, and looked at Esperanza. "Well, what do you think, slave?"

He lowered his head. "Whatever the Mistress wants."

Devona petted Esperanza's hair and then said, "Sorry, Nataya. Maybe another time."

Her reply wasn't what Esperanza expected: he thought Devona would throw him to the lions just for old times' sake. When she stood and he looked in her eyes, he understood why. Devona also noticed how surprised Nataya was to see her. It was the way you looked at a corpse. Nataya thought Devona was already dead.

Mistress Love was wild, but she wasn't crazy, and she certainly wasn't stupid. She knew if she valued her life, it was time to roll and let Esperanza go hunting for Oleksei before the Russians found her first.

Chapter
25

One thing Esperanza could say about Justice was his computer skills were top of the line. He managed to hack into FBI and Interpol databases and retrieve a whole lot of information on Oleksei and his organization.

A former KGB operative, Oleksei turned gangster after the fall of the Soviet Union. Started off as a torpedo, a contract killer, and quickly worked his way up to *avtoritet*—leader. Enjoyed killing and torturing rivals. Got busted for beating a crusading journalist into a coma and did a long stretch in a Russian prison called N-240, which held Russia's most dangerous criminals who weren't condemned to die for their crimes.

After Oleksei was released from N-240, through sheer force of will and ruthlessness, he became one of the biggest and most feared *avtoritets* in the Red Mafiya. His main enterprise was money laundering for Colombian drug cartels and Middle Eastern terrorist cells. Almost every major criminal organization in the States got money laundered by Oleksei and other major Red Mafiya bosses.

Back in Russia, Oleksei and his crew were bumping off

so many people, from government officials to journalists to cops, he was becoming a major headache and drawing way too much attention to the organization, so the Red Mafiya's ruling circle ordered him to leave the country. Deciding it was not profitable to go to war with his powerful brethren, Oleksei relocated to Brighton Beach fifteen years ago and set up shop, though he still operated internationally. The FBI tried to make a case against him several times but witnesses recanted or simply vanished off the face of the earth. Nobody on the inside would ever turn states' evidence because the Russians weren't scared of prison. An American prison was a joke to them.

Esperanza sat on the edge of the desk in his office at Sueño Latino and carefully read through the reports. It made him nervous. If this was the man he'd have to take out, it would be nearly impossible for Havelock and Esperanza to pull it off solo. These weren't some run-of-the-mill drug dealers. Many of Oleksei's men were former soldiers or KGB. Dangerous men. Expert killers. Man had his own private army.

"We're gonna need backup," Esperanza said to Havelock, who was perched on the edge of the leather chair. "Serious guns."

"I hear that. Well, you got the bankroll," he said. "I can get a team together immediately."

Music was coming from downstairs. It was getting harder for Esperanza to make up excuses for where Legs was, and staff kept asking about her. At first, he claimed she was out sick, then he said she'd gotten better but had to go away to deal with some family business. They all knew something was up, but what were they going to say to the club's owner? As long as the new assistant manager kept her head straight, everything would be fine.

"You still got those kind of connections?"

Havelock nodded. "You know me. Never out of the loop." He sat back, whipped out his cell, and crossed his legs. "Don't worry, Nick. I'll get the best of the best."

Esperanza threw the file down on the desk and then massaged his temples.

"You know, when I bought that Lotto ticket, won all that money, and retired from the force, I thought I'd never have to pick up a gun again, except for target practice." Esperanza pulled the 9mm from his hip holster and held it in his open palm. "So much for the wonderful world of retirement."

There was a soft knock. Esperanza quickly put the gun away. Havelock went and opened the door.

"Wassup, baby girl?" Havelock asked.

"I need to speak to Nick."

"C'mon in, Alina," Esperanza said. He was expecting her. He knew sooner or later she'd be asking him questions.

She entered. Seemed jittery.

Havelock said, "I'm gonna go make those phone calls," and stepped out of the office.

"What's goin' on with Legs, Tío?"

"She needed some time to herself."

"Don't bullshit me."

"Okay. Fine. You wanna know the truth, then you need to keep your mouth shut."

"You ain't even gotta say that." She chewed on her thumbnail. Foot tapped the floor.

"She's missing."

"What do you mean?"

"Legs was kidnapped."

"Oh my God." Her eyes got real wide but she managed to keep her composure. "Why the fuck? Who took 'er?"

He didn't want to tell Alina about Devona because he knew she'd only blame herself and it might make her emotionally fall apart, the last thing Esperanza wanted to happen to her. The girl had been through enough. This was his burden to carry. No matter how it turned out, she'd never know it had anything to do with her.

"Don't worry about that. Havelock and I are handling it. I just need you to cover for her. Nobody, and I mean *nobody*, can know about this."

"Anything you need, Tío."

Justice came through with an address for Dragoslav. He lived in a two-bedroom apartment in Brighton Beach. This time, Devona was smart enough to make herself scarce. She wasn't about to walk into the lion's den. Since Dragoslav freelanced and wasn't an actual member of the Russian Mafiya, Esperanza went on his own to see him, while Havelock busied himself putting together a team of professional mercenaries.

Wearing a wool overcoat and a fleece skullcap, Esperanza carefully followed Dragoslav on foot down Brighton Beach Avenue as the B train roared overhead. Esperanza licked his lips. He could taste the salt in the air, since the beach was nearby. The elevated train threw crisscrossing shadows along the pavement and the brick walls and glass fronts of the many mom-and-pop shops lining the avenue. The ground shook for a few moments as Esperanza pretended to make a call from a public phone while keeping his eye on Dragoslav. The Serb was a squat man with a thick beard and a face so flat it was as if it had been bashed in with a metal skillet. Though it was sunny, it was a brisk day, so he wore a leather motorcycle jacket and one of those Russian hats made of thick animal fur. Walked with a limp. *Be easy to make him talk.*

The streets were packed with shoppers. Lots of old ladies with kerchiefs on their heads, using aluminum walkers and wearing mink coats. Funny, when Esperanza went into one of the grocery stores to buy some mints, an old woman in a killer mink coat put her groceries on the counter, said something to the cashier in Russian, and paid with food stamps. All the signs on all the stores were in Russian, except for a damn Starbucks.

Dragoslav was busy shopping. He purchased fruit, black bread, and a bottle of vodka. Chatted and laughed with neighbors. Munched on freshly made *piroshkis*. The scent of butter and onions hung in the air. No wonder they called the neighborhood Little Odessa.

It seemed to take forever, but he finally finished his errands and made his way home.

The building was a four-story tenement. Hallways smelled like Clorox. Esperanza walked up to Dragoslav's door and knocked.

"Yes?"

"Con Edison," Esperanza said. "There's a gas leak and I need to check your stove."

Dragoslav grumbled and then opened the door. Esperanza shoved a gun in his face and pushed his way into the apartment.

"Who are you?" Dragoslav stammered and his dark eyes bulged. "What do you want?"

"We need to talk."

Esperanza grabbed the scared little man by the collar of his flannel shirt and dragged him down the hall to the living room.

When Esperanza entered the cramped, dank living room, he found himself surrounded by four men. Except for the one brandishing a sawed-off shotgun, they all aimed automatic weapons at him. All of them wore shiny silk suits and some had ponytails, reminding Esperanza of bad guys from *Miami Vice*. He immediately got behind Dragoslav and jammed the barrel of his gun against the Serb's temple.

Two other men emerged from the kitchen. Esperanza recognized Oleksei from Russian mug shots. He was older now, late fifties, and bald, with only a wisp of silver hair around his temples. But he had the same fierce look in his blue eyes. His pockmarked face was lengthy and shaped like an upside-down triangle. On his slim, fit physique, he wore an expensive charcoal gray, double-breasted suit made of fine wool.

"You guys make a move and he's dead."

Oleksei pulled a small nickel-plated automatic with a silencer from his suit jacket and shot Dragoslav twice in the chest. Dragoslav's body slumped to the floor.

"Now he is," Oleksei said and flashed big white teeth. "You should not use a worthless minion as a shield. Drop your weapon."

The automatic bounced on the floor. Esperanza kicked it away as he realized Nataya set him and Devona up. Lucky for Devona she didn't tag along, otherwise they'd both be corpses. But how the hell was Esperanza going to get out of this mess? This wasn't Goteri and his clowns. This was a whole other ball game.

"I am Vadim Oleksei. You are a friend of the dominatrix?"

"Not exactly."

"Hired gun, perhaps?"

"Not exactly."

"Not very forthcoming, are you?" Oleksei lowered his weapon and glanced at the older man standing beside him and said something in Russian. The only two words

Esperanza understood were *Devona Love*. At the mention of her name, the other man's face turned beet red and his eyes turned mean.

One of the *byki*—bodyguards—marched over and smashed the butt of his sawed-off shotgun into Esperanza's stomach. He doubled over, and when the butt of the shotgun slammed against the back of his head, he kissed the dirty floor. As he fell into the proverbial black, bottomless pit, he wondered what kind of hell he'd have to face next.

Esperanza heard chatting in Russian. Then laughter. He opened his eyes, the room came into focus, and he found himself in a chair, his hands bound behind his back and his ankles tied to the legs of the chair. This was all too familiar to him and not a good place to be.

Oleksei sat opposite him in a flimsy aluminum folding chair. He puffed on a cigar and blew out circles of smoke while sizing up Esperanza.

"Nicholas Esperanza. The man who took down Bishop." His voice was resonant and there was only a slight trace of an accent. He appeared to be a man who prided himself on eloquence. "Now, why would you be helping Devona Love, since she is your enemy? I heard that she tortured you in ways that no man ever deserved." Oleksei wasn't mocking Esperanza. He was making a statement of fact and chose every word very carefully.

"I didn't have a choice." Esperanza figured it was time to 'fess up. Maybe the truth would set him free. *Yeah, right.* "She's holding my girlfriend hostage."

"Why should I believe you?"

"Because I have no reason to lie."

Oleksei leaned forward and mashed the burning cigar against Esperanza's neck. There was a sizzling sound and stench of burning flesh. Esperanza gritted his teeth and growled, his eyes never leaving Oleksei's. The Russian pulled the cigar away, dropped it on the floor, and crushed it under the sole of his expensive shoes.

"Tough. Good. I admire that quality in a man." He barked something in Russian.

One of his *byki* strolled over, stood behind the chair, firmly grabbed Esperanza's left index finger, and jerked it back until it snapped. Intense, unforgiving pain shot up his arm. It was like ten thousand hot needles and then some. Esperanza let out a half growl, half scream.

"Fuckin' motherfucker. I'm telling you the truth."

"Why are you here?"

"To find out if you're the one who's after Devona and why it is that you want to kill her."

Oleksei nodded. The *byki* broke another finger. Hand and arm on fire, Esperanza growled through clenched teeth, his eyes still never leaving Oleksei's. His adrenaline was pumping now. He could handle whatever pain they dished out. His mind was his greatest weapon.

Oleksei rummaged through his pocket, produced a stick of Double Mint gum, and chewed on it. "And then what?"

Esperanza smirked and said, "I'm going to kill you."

Oleksei threw his head back and let out a laugh. "You and what army? You are nothing. An insignificant ex-*ment*. Ex-cop." He wagged his head in amazement. "Devona obviously has a lot of confidence in you, Mr. Esperanza. You're a hard man. Most Americans, they would've folded by now. Would've been begging. But you can take pain. Should I break another finger? Maybe cut one off this time?"

"What good is that gonna do?"

"Make you tell me where to find Devona."

"If I knew where she was," sweat stung Esperanza's eyes and his broken fingers throb, "I'd find my girlfriend and I'd kill Devona myself. And I wouldn't be here fuckin' around with a bunch of crazy Russians."

"I believe you. But why shouldn't I kill you anyway?"

"Because she gets in contact with me. I can trick her into a meeting. Hand her right over to you. Gift-wrapped. Otherwise she might completely vanish."

Oleksei stroked his chin. Pondered the idea for a moment. "She is quite resourceful, that one."

"She says she's never even met you."

"No. I haven't had the pleasure."

"Then why are you offering all that money to knock her off?"

"Family."

"What do you mean?"

Oleksei glanced at the older man sitting in the battered recliner. He seemed like a peasant. Probably around eighty years old. Round face was a mass of deep wrinkles. White walrus mustache.

"This is Lev. My cousin Anatoliy, who I owe my life to, is married to Lev's daughter Dasha. Lev has three daughters. One of them was raised in France." Oleksei picked lint off his suit jacket. "She became a nun."

The hair on the back of Esperanza's neck stood up. *Sister Terez Mychelle.* It had to be.

"Her birth name was Marina. She changed it to Terez Mychelle Matip, since she wanted to keep her family's ties to organized crime a secret. Lev tells me she was a wonderful woman. Helped the destitute all over Europe. She was given a transfer to an archdiocese in Manhattan. Then, strangely enough, she did not call Lev for a long time. He figured she was busy acclimating herself to her new life in America. He received an occasional letter from her." Oleksei tugged on the cuffs of his shirt and smoothed down his jacket. "About a month ago, a woman's decomposed body was found in la Seine River in Paris. The corpse was in such bad shape it took the police a while to identify her. It was Marina. The French police contacted the NYPD and it seemed a woman had assumed Sister Terez's identity. But the woman disappeared. They thought they'd never find the killer."

"How did you figure out it was Devona?"

"A surveillance video surfaced showing Sister Terez getting into a car with a woman. Lev asked his son-in-law for help to see if the organization could identify her." Oleksei pulled a handkerchief from his back pocket, crossed his legs, and wiped down his polished shoe. "No one knew who she was. Then Dragoslav recognized her. I have been trying to find the elusive witch ever since."

"So this is all about revenge?"

"Yes. Something you should understand. In Russian we call it *razborka*. A settling of accounts."

Lev said something to Oleksei in Russian.

"He said his daughter was a saint. What was done to her should be paid for in blood. He's a good Catholic. Believes in an eye for an eye."

The pain was now a dull throb. Unless Esperanza moved his fingers. "Like I said, I'll bring her to you. Just guarantee my girlfriend's safety."

"You're in no position to ask for anything. Why do I even need you?"

"Because you haven't been able to track her down. And the couple of clowns that did are dead."

"Very well. You will bring Devona to me." The Russian mob boss straightened his silk tie. "Because if you don't? I will kill your entire family. Even your brother, the federal agent." Esperanza cringed. "So your girlfriend's life is the least of your worries."

Though rage swept over him, Esperanza pushed it back and kept his cool. "That's not gonna work for me."

Oleksei shrugged. "Well, I could kill you right now."

Esperanza spat on Oleksei's shoes.

"Well, then fuckin' do it already, you lowlife prick," he said, knowing they might be the last words that he'd ever utter. At this point, he didn't care.

Oleksei glanced down at the gob of saliva on his shoes, smirked, and jammed the barrel of the 9mm against Esperanza's forehead. If he was expecting to see fear in Esperanza's eyes, he could forget about it. He'd danced with the Reaper so many times he didn't fear death anymore. His only regret was not saving Legs. Maybe Havelock would come through.

The smirk vanished from Oleksei's face.

Then he pulled the trigger.

Chapter
26

Santos staked out the apartment building for several boring hours but there'd been no sign of Devona. He debated about going to the apartment and having a look-see but dismissed the idea because he could be putting Legs's life in danger if she was actually being held captive there.

Of course, there was a good chance this was all just a wild goose chase. But his cop's intuition told him otherwise. He always trusted the old gut, why change now?

He shuddered, trying to shake off a chill. Though it was spring, the temperature had dropped to nearly winter digits again. Santos poured black coffee from his thermos into a plastic cup and took a sip. He wished he could turn on the heat, but he couldn't afford to leave the motor running since he'd be easier to spot.

A Lexus sedan with tinted windows pulled up in front of the building. Santos slunk low and picked up his light-weight field glasses and checked out the vehicle. His heart was racing. Wasn't sure why.

He punched the dashboard when he saw two clean-cut white guys emerge from the car. They laughed and kissed on the lips and strolled to the building hand in hand. So much for that.

Santos placed the field glasses on his lap and pulled the brim of his hat low over his eyes and sipped his *café*.

He hated stakeouts.

"You're lucky to be alive," Havelock said as he stepped on the gas and raced along the Brooklyn-Queens Expressway. He glanced at the cigar burn on Esperanza's neck.

Esperanza's broken fingers were wrapped tightly with a bandana. He stared straight ahead, his expression stoic.

"Everybody thought that I was the luckiest guy in the world when I won the Lotto?" he said, his voice raspy. "Bullshit. Oleksei's gun jamming? Now that makes me the luckiest fucker in the world. And it didn't hurt that the old man, Lev, is a believer in fate. He figured I'd been touched by grace somehow. Convinced Oleksei *not* to finish me off and give me a chance to bring Devona in." Esperanza barely moved any part of his body. The electric shocks from his broken fingers had greatly intensified. His burnt skin was on fire. His ribs and jaw also ached. The vicodin helped only a little. Esperanza pushed the pain out of his mind as he stared at his hand. His fingers were blue and swollen like sausages. He moved them slightly and clenched his teeth.

Own this, Nick. Own the pain. It's not gonna stop you from doing what you gotta do.

Oleksei ordered his crew to give Esperanza a beat down, just to make sure he got the message: *Don't fuck with Vadim Oleksei.* So a barrage of punches and kicks were ruthlessly doled out. Fists and heels to his head. His face. His stomach. And they laughed while doing it.

After the Russians dragged him outside and unceremoniously threw him behind the dumpster of a fish store,

Esperanza phoned Havelock to come get him since he couldn't stand up, let alone drive.

As Havelock got on the Brooklyn Bridge, Esperanza leaned his head back against the headrest. The bright lights of Manhattan were like a beacon. Esperanza fuckin' hated Brooklyn. Nothing good had ever happened to him there.

"You shouldn't have gone alone."

"Yeah, well a little late now," Esperanza said while he stroked his swollen jaw. He lost a couple of teeth. At least they were molars and not his front teeth. He was also lucky his jaw wasn't broken. *Probably 'cause they went easy on me.* "You know the other reason I think Oleksei didn't finish me off? He was impressed by the fact that I didn't flinch when he pulled the trigger. I didn't fear death. He seems to admire that quality in a man."

"I can't wait to see if he flinches when we pump him full of bullets."

"We have six hours to bring him Devona."

Esperanza got lucky his brains weren't splattered all over Dragoslav's living room. Now he needed to play the last hand just right. The one advantage Esperanza had was the fact that Oleksei was so damn overconfident. He didn't see Esperanza as any kind of real threat.

I will kill your entire family.

That warning was supposed to keep Esperanza in check. Fill him with fear. The mistake Oleksei made was, now Esperanza was committed to killing the Russian and all of his men, no matter what it took. No matter what the consequences.

It was the only way the ruthless gangster's promise would never be fulfilled.

The next move was to get Esperanza's injuries treated. Get his digits x-rayed, set, and splinted. Then get ready for a violent showdown. Luckily, Esperanza was good friends with Dr. Bob Donato at Saint Vincent's Hospital. He'd already made the call, since he needed to get in and out as quickly as possible.

Esperanza was exhausted and pumped up at the same time. Adrenaline was the ultimate drug.

"What if Devona doesn't call within the time frame?" Havelock asked as he weaved through the West Side Highway traffic and the SUV's speedometer hit seventy mph.

"She will. She knows I was going to see Dragoslav."

"When she does, are you gonna tell her the truth?"

"Hell no. I'm gonna set her up."

"And when we deliver her to Oleksei, what happens to Legs?"

Ripples of nausea swept over Esperanza. His head went into a tailspin. He lowered the window, leaned his head out, and gulped down cold air.

The situation was grave, and he was uncertain about how it was going to turn out, and who would pay with their life.

Esperanza was willing to die for Legs. In a heartbeat. But he wouldn't be able to live with himself if he didn't manage to save her.

You will. No matter what it takes, Legs will come out of this safe and sound.

He wasn't sure why, but it made him angry with his friend for asking the question about Legs in the first place. Esperanza leaned back and closed the car's window.

"I really don't know, Havelock. I'm trying to work this thing out as I go along."

Santos didn't realize that he'd dozed off until the roar of a passing garbage truck jolted him from his unintended nap. He rubbed his burning, tired eyes. Maybe this whole thing was just a dead end.

The hairs on the nape of his neck stood up when he noticed a woman in a long leather coat and bowler hat get out of a car. Expensive sedan. Expensive broad. She cautiously scoped out the street. Santos quickly picked up his field glasses and took a look. He slunk lower in his seat.

Jackpot.

Mistress Devona Love.

She strutted to the building's entrance, cautiously glanced around again. Oddly enough, she didn't go inside the building. She continued walking and went down the steps of the building's service entrance.

Why?

Santos decided to sit tight and not follow her. He'd wait awhile and see if she left again, then go see what was up.

He picked up his cell and was about to dial Esperanza, then changed his mind. He'd promised Nicholas he'd stay out of it, and Santos was a man who always kept his word. Besides, he'd call Esperanza when he was certain about Legs.

Good news was, at least Santos knew where Devona was holed up, so she wasn't getting away this time.

The assault team assembled at Mitchell Laight's loft in Williamsburg, Brooklyn, a vast space lit by harsh overhead lights. There was a minimal amount of furniture, all secondhand stuff, and the brick walls were spray-painted metallic silver. It really didn't feel like a living space.

Mitchell grinned as he rushed over to Esperanza and gave him a megahug.

"Nick, you bastard," Mitchell said. "It's good to see you."

Esperanza smiled and patted his old SEAL team member on the face. He was glad to have him aboard. Mitchell was an expert sniper.

"Wish it could be under better circumstances," Mitchell said. A Southern boy, Mitchell still reminded Esperanza of the All-American football player: neatly trimmed blond hair parted to the side, to die for blue eyes, and a jaw so square it could star in its own comic book.

"Yeah." Esperanza wished the same thing. Mitchell wore his usual civilian outfit: black T-shirt, straight-leg Levi's washed to near extinction, and scuffed motorcycle boots.

"Thanks for helping out."

"Anything for you, Nick." Mitchell glanced at Esperanza's hand, his bandaged neck, and his swollen jaw. There was a flicker of anger in his indigo eyes. "Meet the rest of the crew."

Three other men were sitting at an expansive table, which had been sanded down to bare wood.

"Jim Shell. Former Delta Force Operator." Shell stood up and did the whole military salute thing, which Esperanza found a bit odd. He was a black man with cinnamon-hued skin and hair buzzed short, military style. Seemed to be in his mid thirties. "At your service, sir." He was of medium height and wide build and had a pleasant, broad face. Esperanza reluctantly saluted Shell, then shook his hand.

"We're all just a bunch of civilians here, Shell."

"Once a soldier, always a soldier," Shell said, voice brimming with pride.

Esperanza really couldn't argue with that.

The second man stood up. His curly red hair was badly in need of a trim, and a mass of freckles dotted his oval face. A jagged scar snaked along the edge of his jaw. Slender. Barely thirty.

"Tim Jenkins," he said. He had a Midwestern accent. "Former US Navy SEAL shooter. I'm honored to meet you."

"Glad to have you aboard."

"Now that we got the intros out the way, let's get to it," Havelock said, all business. Except this was the business of killing.

Esperanza was impressed that Havelock managed to put together such a serious crew on such short notice. On their drive to Williamsburg, Havelock filled Esperanza in on their military experience, and these guys were an impressive group of soldiers. It reignited Esperanza's confidence that they'd be able to pull this whole thing off.

They all sat at the table. Mitchell immediately opened his laptop and started typing.

Though there were only five of them, if they planned this right, they'd be able to take on a whole lot of Russian gangsters.

"How many guns are we looking at?"

Esperanza shrugged. "Not sure. Could be five. Could be ten. Depends on how confident Oleksei is."

"So the other major question is the location," Mitchell said. "That's going to really determine how to run this operation."

"And what equipment we're gonna need," Havelock added.

Mitchell grinned again. "Whatever we need, trust me, I have it available."

Esperanza had been giving the location of the meet some serious thought. He needed to pick the spot, no matter what Oleksei demanded.

What was the biggest advantage his assault team had? *Invisibility.*

"How about a wide-open space?" Esperanza said.

"Like?" Havelock asked.

"The beach," Mitchell said. "Before dawn."

Havelock smirked. "Perfect."

"I'm downloading satellite maps as we speak," Mitchell said.

The rest of the men nodded. Esperanza felt a sense of relief, even confidence. Now all they needed was to come up with a solid plan of attack.

Chapter
27

"Seems like we're close to a resolution," Devona said as she sashayed into the cage. All black, leather cat suit and matching knee-high boots and ankle-length coat.

Legs was sitting on the cot, hands resting on her knees, head demurely lowered.

"What's going on?"

Devona angled forward, tenderly placed her fingers under Legs's chin, and pulled her head up. "Nicholas wants me to meet him. Said that Dragoslav gave him a solid lead. We actually might find out who is really behind this." She caressed Legs's cheek with the back of her hand. "Then all your boyfriend has to do is kill the bastard."

"He'll do whatever it takes to save me." Legs said the words as a simple matter of fact.

"I'm counting on that." Devona placed the palm of her hand behind Legs's head and drew her forward and kissed her deeply. There was such tenderness in the kiss, Legs got this strange feeling, as if Devona was saying good-bye. Devona pulled away slightly, but remained close enough for Legs to feel her warm breath, which smelled of expensive champagne. "At the same time, I'm a little mistrusting, so if Otto doesn't hear from me, in let's say three hours . . ." She squeezed Legs's face hard. "He's been ordered to snap your neck."

Legs swallowed. Her body became rigid. Either she'd soon be set free, or she was going to die.

"I'll pray for your soul."

Devona chuckled. "Don't bother. When I lost Jason, I lost my soul, anyway. Until I get my revenge, I won't be satisfied."

"Revenge won't bring him back."

"But it'll make me feel much better." She gave Legs a condescending pat on the face. "So even if you get out of this predicament now, I'll be back sooner than you think."

At Mitchell's loft, Esperanza watched as Havelock and the crew checked the weapons before they finished loading up the two nondescript cargo vans.

Havelock, wearing tan army fatigues, slapped a magazine into his MK 11 SWS. Sniper weapon system. It was strange to see the big man in battle dress again. But, hey, they were going off to a little private war, weren't they?

"Is that the same weapon from back in the day?" Esperanza asked.

"Damn straight," Havelock said, holding up the perfectly maintained .30 cal semiauto rifle.

Mitchell chuckled. "I see you're still old school." He flipped open a case, pulled out a spanking-new weapon, and showed it off. "Here's the new shit, pardner. Knight's Armament Stoner Rifle-25. SR-25 for short."

Havelock took it, held it, and aimed the semiauto at

the wall. "Nice balance. Lightweight." He handed it back to Mitchell. "Still prefer my ol'-school shit."

"Well, this baby did wonders for me while I was in Afghanistan," Mitchell said.

"You were a soldier for hire?" Esperanza asked.

"Shit, half the troops in the Middle East conflicts are for hire," Havelock said.

"And, trust me, they get paid a lot better than the government troops." Mitchell placed a scope on the SR-25. "Damn shame."

Esperanza slipped on body armor as he watched Shell and Jenkins at the other end of the table changing into wet suits. "I hope I'm payin' you enough."

"I'm not takin' a damn dime from you, Nick." Mitchell grinned as he slapped a magazine into his sniper rifle. "This one's for friendship."

Santos switched parking spaces, since he knew he couldn't be too careful. Last thing he wanted was to be spotted. He watched Devona emerge from the side of the building. She got in her car and drove off.

He waited for several minutes. Took out his Glock semiautomatic and checked it. He missed the classic Smith & Wesson .38 caliber revolvers. To Santos, they were more reliable than the semiautos. But what difference did it make? In his thirty years on the job, he'd never actually fired his weapon, and he wanted to keep it that way. He slipped the gun back in his belt holster, climbed out of his car, opened the trunk, took out a crowbar, slipped it under his coat, and headed to the building's service entrance.

Now he'd find out if his instincts were right. The wind wailed as if it was a victim calling out for help. Santos thought about Legs and shuddered. He was anxious, and though he hated to admit it, he was a little scared, too. Because he had no idea what he might have to face. No partner. No backup. He was on his own.

Santos marched down the steps to the basement entrance, stopped for a moment, pulled a small flashlight, and turned it on.

Light severed the darkness and Santos said a silent little prayer.

Though it took some convincing, Oleksei agreed to meet Esperanza at Brighton Beach at four a.m. Esperanza had counted on Oleksei believing that such an open space would give him the upper hand, because there was no way for Esperanza to set up any kind of ambush. Little did the Russian know that sand and surf and the cover of darkness were a SEAL's best friend.

By the time Esperanza made the call to Oleksei, the team was already in place.

Now it was time to deal with Devona.

Parked under the FDR near the Brooklyn Bridge, across from the Alfred Smith housing projects, Esperanza watched in the rearview mirror as headlight beams gradually approached. There wasn't a soul around the desolate area, which was why he asked Devona to meet him there in the first place. He was dressed in a black turtleneck, black cargo pants, combat boots, and a leather jacket. Also, light body armor.

He got out of the car and watched Devona strut over, flashing her usual arrogant smile.

He couldn't wait to wipe that smile off her face.

"Well, what's the situation?" she asked, hands tucked in the pockets of her coat. She glanced at his left hand, his fingers in a splint. "What happened to you?"

Now it was Esperanza's turn to smile. Devona abruptly stopped, confused by his condescending expression. She was about to say something when Esperanza delivered a wicked right hook to her jaw and the impact of the blow made her stumble backward. Esperanza never hit a woman before, but Devona was a whole different story. Talk about someone who had it coming. Hitting her actually turned him on. Maybe it was a little perverse, but he didn't have time to question his emotions. He was going to be in control now. Devona almost dropped to her knees and placed her hand on the trunk of Esperanza's car to regain her balance. Her free hand was reaching for something underneath her coat. She managed to pull out a nickel-plated .22 but Esperanza trapped her wrist and twisted counterclockwise, forcing her to drop the gun, then he slipped behind her, hooked his arm around her neck, and placed her in a sleeper hold. She struggled to break free and the more she struggled, the more aroused he became. *How you like me now, bitch?* Those violent erotic dreams he'd told Dr. Yuen about flashed in his mind.

After a few seconds, Devona's body went limp as she lost consciousness.

Esperanza took a moment to regain control of his emotions. Kept hearing Havelock's words. Thought about the men prepared to fight and die for him. They were soldiers and he was one, too.

He opened the back door and shoved her in the car face first. He used plasticuffs to bind her hands behind her back. He also bound her ankles, since he had no intention of getting kicked in back of the head with those stilleto heels if she woke up during the ride to Brooklyn. He jerked her coat over her head and thoroughly frisked her. She had another .22 tucked in the small of her back. That was it.

As he drove up the ramp to the Brooklyn Bridge, Esperanza glanced over his shoulder at Devona on the floor of the car. He had no intention of handing her over to Oleksei. Oleksei and his men had to die. There was no doubt in his mind.

Then Devona would either give up Legs's location or he'd torture her. Either way, she was going to tell him, since he got the feeling she wouldn't be able to take the kind of pain she was always so eager to dish out.

If she didn't talk, for once, Mistress Devona Love would be the one screaming for mercy.

Using the crowbar and all the strength he could muster, Santos managed to get the basement door open. He made more noise than he wanted to, but unfortunately, he didn't have Esperanza's lock-picking skills.

Santos drew his gun, stepped into the darkness, and methodically made his way down a lengthy hallway. He could hear the hum of a massive boiler. He entered a dank, cavernous space. There were cement beams and water pipes snaking along the low, asbestos-covered ceiling. Piles of large black garbage bags seemed to be everywhere, filling the air with the sickening stench of rotting food. Santos kept searching, and then found another door that said KEEP OUT. He put his gun away and got to work with the crowbar once again.

A harsh metallic sound jolted Legs from her sleep. Sounded like someone was breaking in. Her heart did a wild conga solo as she cautiously tiptoed to the cage door, held on to the bars, peeked out, and saw a flashlight beam coming down the metal stairs.

Is this another one of Devona's mind games? Get me all excited, making me think someone is coming to rescue me?

The beam of light blinded her and Legs squinted as she heard footsteps coming closer and closer.

"Legs?"

It was Santos's resonant voice. He lowered the flashlight and now she could see him. Was he a mirage? Was she hallucinating? It was like her guardian angel had suddenly appeared to rescue her. Her grip tightened and she pressed her face harder between the metal bars. Santos was holding a gun in one hand and had a crowbar tucked under his arm. But where was Nick? Why would he send his ex-partner by himself? And if Nick knew where she was, why didn't he come himself to free her?

"Anibal!"

"Are you okay?"

"Yeah. Get me the hell out of here."

"Step back."

She did, and he put the gun and the flashlight in his coat pocket. He slipped the tip of the crowbar between the cage door and the lock and gritted his teeth as he pulled it back. There was a creaky whine and then the cage door popped open.

Freedom.

Legs's sense of relief immediately vanished when she saw Otto's gigantic shadow looming on the wall behind Santos. She tried to scream to warn him, but no sound came out of her mouth. Santos must've noticed the shocked expression on her face, because he quickly reeled around. The next thing he knew, Otto's massive hand clutched his neck. The giant easily lifted Santos off the ground and then began to choke the life out of him.

Chapter

28

Seemed like Coney Island Avenue in Brooklyn would never end. It finally did. Ironically, it didn't end at Coney Island but at Brighton Beach instead. Esperanza parked his car on Brighton Fifteenth Street. They were a few blocks away from the next-to-last entrance to Brighton Beach. He turned off the ignition and heard Devona stir awake.

He turned around, looked over his shoulder and said, "Good morning, sunshine."

She craned her head so she could see between the seats, looking none too happy. "What the fuck are you trying to pull here?" The words sounded almost like an animal growling. "You screwed up big time."

"Shut the fuck up."

He gave her the lowdown of what was going to happen and why. She went ballistic. Cursed and screamed like a banshee. Banged her head against the back seat. Her body went into wild convulsions and she made all kinds of crazy threats.

Esperanza remained perfectly calm, got out of the car,

opened the back door, and said, "You better stay chill. If not, I'm gonna hurt you," and then dragged her out of the car and cut the plasticuffs from her ankles, but not her wrists. "Don't worry, sweetheart. I'll protect you."

"Like you protected Legs?" She raised an eyebrow, expression filled with sarcasm.

He grabbed her by the arm and roughly shook her. "You either walk with me or I'll drag your ass. Make a choice."

"Walking sounds much better."

There was no moon and barely a star in the sky. In the darkness he couldn't even see the ocean, but he could hear the waves as they crashed against the surf, and an aggressive breeze occasionally blew stinging clouds of sand into the air. Esperanza pulled Devona along, his three good fingers clutched around her arm while his good hand held an automatic at his side. She was having a difficult time walking on the sand since she was wearing stilettos, and the weight of the body armor under her coat probably didn't help much, either.

For a moment, Esperanza thought about throwing her over his shoulder and carrying her, just to humiliate her, but she was a substantial girl and it would only end up tiring him out and slowing him down.

"Just do as I say and you'll be fine."

The meeting spot Esperanza chose was Brightwater Avenue. The beach ended there, cut off by a cement divider. On the other side of the divider there were four, two-story family houses and a six-story apartment building. Oleksei found the meeting place acceptable because he thought it would be extremely difficult to ambush him and his men.

Headlights turned off the street. A Mercedes and two Escalade SUVs bumped their way down wide concrete steps, then onto the boardwalk and finally onto the sand. They stopped, headlights making it a bit difficult for Esperanza and Devona to see. Twelve men, including Oleksei and Lev, confidently climbed out of the vehicles. Headlights stayed on, harsh white beams slashing the darkness. Though they were silhouettes, Esperanza could see that the bodyguards wore silk double-breasted suits and fancy leather shoes and brandished machine pistols. Behind the Russians were the houses. To their right was a parking lot they'd probably checked out already, to their left the empty ocean, and in front of them an open beach where Esperanza was standing with the prize everyone wanted.

They held all the cards. Had all the strategic advantages.

"All of this 'cause of a nun, huh?" Devona asked.

"Yeah." Esperanza snorted. "You sure know how to pick 'em."

Forty feet away from Oleksei, Esperanza and Devona stopped.

"Very good, Mr. Esperanza," Oleksei shouted. "I'm glad you took me seriously. Bring Devona to me."

"I don't think so."

Oleksei glanced at his men. "Don't be foolish. We can gun you down right now, but I want her alive."

"And I want you dead."

Suddenly, there was a noise in the sky. A loud, incessant buzzing. All of Oleksei's men looked toward the dark heavens wondering what the hell was producing the sound.

"Close your eyes," Esperanza said to Devona.

"Why?"

"Just do it."

Devona obeyed. Though it was nearly impossible to see, Esperanza knew it was a three-foot-long, radio-controlled model replica of a Black Hawk attack helicopter that hovered over Oleksei and his crew. Mitchell's brilliant little idea.

The mobsters were uncertain of what it was and were about to shoot it down when Esperanza suddenly shoved Devona to the sand, dove on top of her, and clamped his eyes shut. He heard the flash grenade attached to the Black Hawk go off and knew there was a bright flash of light that left the Russians blind.

Then the bullets started to fly.

Santos bounced off the concrete wall and landed on his back on the damp floor. He chomped down on his bent index finger to keep himself from screaming, the pain was so intense. He looked up in time to see the giant marching his way. Santos managed to pull his Glock, but a humongous foot kicked it out of his hand and it slid across the cement floor and out of sight.

"Otto! No!" Legs shouted.

Unfortunately, the giant paid no attention, bent over, grabbed Santos by the collar of his coat, and hauled him up. Face-to-face with a giant with a leather mask and cold blue eyes, Santos tried to punch him, but his reach wasn't long enough. Otto pulled him close and head-butted him square in the face. There were bright flashes of light and Santos couldn't breathe through his nose, which was probably broken, and he knew that one more blow like that? He was done for.

A shot rang out.

* * *

Otto quickly turned around, startled by the sound of gun-fire, but he still didn't let Santos free from his powerful grasp. A semiconscious Santos squinted.

Legs raised Santos's Glock and aimed it at Otto.

"Please, Otto," she said, her voice and hands incredibly steady. "I don't want to hurt you." She prayed that Otto didn't decide to use Santos as a shield, since she wasn't a great shot.

Otto punched Santos across the temple and dropped him. Even Legs was able to figure out that he wasn't a professional criminal when he literally had a hostage in his hands and didn't use that to his advantage. Or did Otto believe that Legs was incapable of hurting him?

Santos was splayed out, choking on his own blood, which he spit up. He rolled on his stomach and attempted to get to his feet, but the ground seemed to keep slipping from underneath him. He watched as Otto very slowly strode toward Legs, held out his hand and said, "Give me the gun."

Legs could see it in Santos' desperate eyes: the last thing he wanted was for Legs to kill a man. She knew that in all his years as a cop, Santos never had to live with that burden, so why should she? But what could he do to stop it? She was on her own. She had the power now and Otto understood that, which was probably why he was taking baby steps and not charging at her.

Nice as he treated her, she was ready to put a bullet between his eyes.

Esperanza dragged Legs to the shooting range a few times and taught her the basics of using a firearm, just in case the day ever came when she had to defend herself with a gun. On one of those afternoons, Esperanza told her, "The first time you kill a man? Everything changes. Hearing their last breath, watching their eyes grow dim, a part of you dies with them. And it's something you can never take back." Legs didn't want a man's blood on her hands, but Santos's life was on the line, so what she wanted didn't matter. She had to save her friend. And herself.

Her feet were about shoulder width apart and her lead leg was slightly bent, her finger relaxed on the trigger. She kept her eyes on the target. Legs carefully aimed at Otto's chest, since she'd less likely miss. A head shot would be much tougher.

She took a deep breath as the giant stepped closer.

Several hundred feet behind Devona and Esperanza, flanking them, the barrels of sniper rifles emerged from underneath the sand like coiled cobras ready to strike.

Havelock and Mitchell.

They began picking off the blinded Russian gangsters, who fired their weapons in different directions hoping to nail their invisible adversaries.

Then, from the dark, ominous ocean, more gunfire erupted and Red Mafiya soldiers went down like they were stationary targets at a firing range. Black-as-night blood squirted from heads and chests, and bodies doubled over and flipped and collapsed in rapid succession in an almost surreal dance of death.

Still lying on top of Devona, Esperanza lifted his head and squinted as puffs of sand sprayed from the ricochet of bullets all around them. He aimed his weapon and calmly placed Oleksei in his sights. He fired. The first shot missed. A headlight exploded. The second shot nailed the bastard in the stomach. The third one hit Oleksei in the neck. He clutched his neck, twirled around, and dropped to the ground as he continued firing his automatic.

The whole gun battle took less than two minutes. All the Russians were dead. Esperanza stood up and lifted Devona to her feet. For once, she appeared startled and confused.

"How the fuck?"

From the ocean waves, Jenkins and Shell appeared. They wore wet suits and swept the barrels of their machine pistols methodically from side to side, making sure none of the targets were still alive. They'd been positioned on black rubber rafts several yards out in the ocean.

"Invisibility," Esperanza said and looked over his shoulder.

Havelock and Mitchell, wearing beige camouflage uniforms and brandishing sniper rifles with night-vision scopes, also marched forward. They'd both been buried lying face down in a shallow foxhole, hidden under blankets covered by sand, with only enough of an opening for the barrel of their rifles to stick out, and so far away there was no way for anyone to see them.

"You don't fuck around, do you?" Devona said, obviously impressed by the massacre she'd just witnessed.

"You should've figured that one out a long time ago."

Esperanza grabbed her arm and dragged her toward the crew of dead Russians, Havelock and Mitchell walking alongside them.

Santos suddenly remembered that he carried a backup weapon. Too bad it wasn't a gun. But it would have to do. Santos searched his coat pocket, found the foam grip of the telescoping steel baton, and pulled it out.

His body was numb from the pain. It was like he got hit by a friggin' truck. He crawled and wondered if he could pull it off. He should've never tried to go at this alone.

I'm just a murder cop, used to dealing with forensic evidence and interviewing witnesses, not hand-to-hand combat.

Thankfully, Otto hesitated enough to give Santos a little time. The big mook could tell that Legs meant business, yet chose not to use Santos as a human shield. Very strange.

Santos didn't know how he found the strength, but he managed to get in a crouch. With the click of the release, the baton extended to twenty-one inches. Santos dove, swung the baton, and slammed it behind Otto's right knee, forcing the giant to drop to one knee.

Before Otto could turn around, Santos, both of his hands securely gripping the baton, swung fast and hard and smashed steel against the back of Otto's head. The giant found himself on his knees. He groaned like some kind of wounded jungle cat and struggled to get back on his feet. Legs rushed over and pistol-whipped the giant like she was a pro. Santos, still kneeling, raised the baton high over his head and whacked Otto once more. Between the two of them, they finally managed to put Otto's lights out. His massive body fell face forward to the ground. Santos slid back, relaxed, and let out a slightly nervous giggle. The building with feet was finally down for the count.

He looked up at Legs, his vision still a little blurry. She was one cool chick. "I heard you *barrio* girls were hardcore, but damn, *mami*."

She held her hand out, which he immediately took, and Legs hauled him to his feet.

"Can you walk?" she asked.

"Barely." She draped his arm over her shoulder, helped him walk, and kept the automatic leveled, hand still stable, as they headed for the stairs. "When I worked this out in my head, *I* was the one who was supposed to save *you*."

She gave him a warm kiss on the cheek as her eyes filled with tears. "Save me, you did, *papito*. I owe you *por vida*—for life."

They hurriedly made their way up the metal stairs.

Oleksei was still alive. Barely. The neck wound was only a graze, but he'd soon bleed out from the hollow-point-bullet wound to the stomach. Esperanza inhaled the crisp, salty air and glanced over at Lev's twisted corpse. The top of the old man's head had been blown off. He was clutching a rosary in his dead hand. Esperanza kneeled down and closed Lev's eyes since he felt a little bad for him. All he wanted was justice for his daughter, and he paid with his life instead.

Because of Devona.

All of this mayhem. Bullets, blood, and death.

Because of Devona.

There was a wheezing sound. Esperanza stared down at Oleksei, who smiled with a mouth full of blood.

"I should have killed you while I had the chance," he said. "Never let sentimentality mix with business."

"And you should never threaten a man's family." Esperanza aimed his 9mm at Oleksei. Turned to Devona, stared into her eyes as he shot the Russian gangster. "Now you and I are going for a little ride." He looked back down at Oleksei. There was a large hole right between his blank eyes. Blood oozed down the side of his head and was swallowed up by the sand.

Esperanza looked up at Devona, who was still staring at Oleksei. She gulped and the color drained from her face. Was it fear that he sensed? She closed her eyes for a long moment. He wondered if Devona was praying for her life. Highly unlikely. Probably trying to figure out how she was going to weasel her way out of this predicament. But there was no way out this time.

"Charges are set," Havelock said. They placed explosives around the cars. The less evidence left behind, the better.

"Let's go, then."

Esperanza grabbed Devona's arm, pulled her close, and they walked away, followed by Havelock and the rest of the assault team. As soon as they got to the vans and Esperanza's car, Havelock pressed the detonator and for a moment, night turned into day as huge explosions rocked Brighton Beach. The cars would burn.

So would the dead bodies.

With Santos's arm still draped around her shoulder, Legs helped him cross the street to his car. He was limping and then he stumbled, so she had to stop for a moment to regain her balance. She glanced around, couldn't believe she was outside. Took a deep breath. The air smelled so clean. A couple of cool raindrops spattered against her face. She was alive. She was free. Made her want to scream for joy.

For a moment, back in the basement, she was actually going to shoot Otto. She was glad that Santos stopped her. Otto had only been a pawn in Devona's twisted game. But Legs also thought, what would it have felt like to take a person's life for real? If Devona had been there, she would've known. No doubt.

As Legs helped a disoriented Santos get in the passenger seat of his car, she said, "We have to get in touch with Nicholas right away."

Chapter
29

A steady rain was falling as Esperanza parked his car by the West Side Pier walkway, near the meatpacking district. They weren't very far from the very same warehouse where he first encountered Devona and Rybak.

Where the nightmare had started, and where it all was going to end.

Devona's hands were still bound behind her back as she sat in the passenger seat next to him.

Her face turned red as Esperanza strangled her.

Though he was choking the life out of her, her eyes remained defiant. He wanted to finish her off. Wanted her dead. He got control of his rage and released his grip. Devona coughed and fought to catch her breath.

How does it feel, Mistress Love?

"Where is she?"

Esperanza's cell phone vibrated. He looked at the caller ID. It was Santos. Last person in the world he wanted to talk to. He put the cell on the dashboard, grabbed Devona by the hair, jerked her head back, then reached into his boot, whipped out a pearl-handle switchblade, flicked it open, jammed the tip right under her left eye, and drew blood.

"Start talking or I start cutting off pieces of your face."

"I'm not scared of you, Nicholas," Devona said. "If Legs were dead, I probably would be. But no matter how badly you want to kill me, you won't sacrifice her."

She was right on that count. But there were other options.

"Do you think you're the only one with a gift for torture?" he asked as he twisted the knife and made her wince. "How much pain do you think you could handle before I make you talk?"

"All you got is fifteen minutes. If I don't call in to Otto, your girlfriend's toast."

Though he knew she might be bluffing, he wasn't willing to take that chance. The time frame seemed pretty accurate. And Devona was the type to always have a backup plan.

He pulled the knife away and there was a small puncture wound under her eye. A trickle of red snaked down her cheek and it seemed as if she was crying tears of blood.

"Lean forward," Esperanza said. She did. He cut the plasticuffs. She rubbed her sore wrists. "Now call Otto and set up an exchange. I get Legs, you get to live."

"That's acceptable."

"It better be."

She reached into her coat pocket, took out her cell phone, and dialed. The phone rang several times, but no one answered. Devona glanced at Esperanza and shrugged. She seemed anxious. Kept tugging on a strand of hair. Devona redialed.

Esperanza's phone vibrated again and he grabbed it. Santos. But this time it wasn't a voice message. It was a text message. When Esperanza saw the words on the screen, he swore his heart actually skipped a beat.

Legs is OK. She's with me. Call ASAP.

Esperanza put the phone away and let out a small chuckle as he turned and stared at Devona, who confidently spoke into her own cell phone.

"Yes, Otto. I want you to bring her to the meatpacking district . . ."

Such a fine actress.

Esperanza snatched the phone from her hand and brought it to his ear. Nothing. He smiled as he threw it on her lap.

"You're through, Devona. Legs ain't with Otto anymore." He drew his gun and aimed it at her. She bit her bottom lip. Cheeks flushed. Now she seemed genuinely scared, and that expression on her face got Esperanza extremely aroused. "Take off the body armor and get out of the fucking car."

Devona was a few feet ahead of Esperanza, marching down the walkway that jutted forty feet out to the Hudson River. This was a place where families congregated during the day and crews of gay men played at night. It was five in the morning and because of the downpour, it was deserted. Across the river, Jersey was dark. A powerful gust of wind blew off the Hudson. Devona's stiletto heels made loud clunky sounds on the wooden planks, which was accompanied by the plop, plop of raindrops.

Dead woman walking, Esperanza thought.

"You can't kill me," Devona said as she glanced over her shoulder.

"What makes you think that?"

She stopped at the end of the walkway and turned around. "It would be like killing a part of yourself."

"Not much of a price to pay for peace of mind." Out of nowhere Esperanza produced a combat knife and threw it. It twirled through the air at high speed and landed right between Devona's feet, tip stuck in the wooden plank. She glanced down at the knife, seemed quite surprised, maybe even a little confused. "Pick it up."

She squatted and jerked the knife from the wood, held it up, and admired it while simultaneously checking out the weapon's balance. The knife had a polymer grip, metal guard, and butt cap, and a gleaming, seven-inch, partially serrated blade made of stainless steel. Devona seemed to be getting turned on by the quality of the weapon. She stared at Esperanza and smirked. He could see it in her eyes, she was hot and bothered, which meant she was probably experienced in the use of a combat knife.

"I guess we have some kind of challenge here?"

"You get past me, you're free to go."

"And what's your weapon, if I might ask?"

"Bare hands."

"Even with the broken fingers? Confident, aren't we?"

"Determined is a better word."

She licked the edge of the blade. "And if I don't make it past you?"

"You die."

"Kind of unfair odds, don't you think?"

"You that good with a knife?" He stepped forward.

"Second nature." She twirled the blade. Held it and waved it around, then took a defensive position. A hammer grip and triangle stance. Free hand was open, held up at her shoulder while the knife was at her waist and held outward. Nothing fancy but very effective. Meant she knew her shit. Rybak had taught her well. Esperanza raised his hands and they began to circle each other. "You know, thought you were gonna shoot me. Didn't think you'd want to kill me with your bare hands."

"Back to basics."

She feigned a stab to his left side and then slashed across his right. Razor-sharp blade sliced across his shoulder. Left a three-inch cut that took a couple of seconds to bleed.

"That's gotta hurt."

He did a fast leg sweep. Devona hopped over his leg, and as her feet touched the ground, she brought the knife down in an overhead stab. He parried with his right forearm, and then landed a hook kick to the small of her back, which sent her stumbling forward, but she quickly regained her composure. Even though Esperanza knew he'd hurt her, she didn't waste any time and immediately counterattacked. With the rain in his eyes, Devona sometimes seemed like a blur. She delivered a quick uppercut stab. He blocked her, but then she slammed her knee into his already fractured ribs. Almost punched his clock. The ribs were definitely broken now, and breathing seemed nearly impossible.

As Devona stabbed and slashed, forcing him back toward the parking lot, Esperanza started to think that maybe this was not such a good idea: he should've shot the bitch in the head and finished it. After the beat down he received from the Russian gangsters, his body wasn't exactly operating at hundred percent.

Quick feet, Esperanza. Dance.

He glided around her, bobbing and weaving. The wood was slippery from the rain, but luckily his boots had a good rubber grip. He was amazed that Devona managed to not slip and fall in spite of her stilettos.

Devona shrieked as she swung from left to right, attempting to cut his carotid artery. Esperanza leaned back and the tip of the blade barely missed his neck. He spun counterclockwise and smashed her across the jaw with a wicked back fist, which left her disoriented and off balance.

He caught her right forearm and was about to twist it when Devona bashed her left elbow on his broken fingers. It almost made him cry out—it felt like someone just shoved his hand into a pot of boiling water, and the pain made him let go of Devona.

They stalked each other again, carefully circling, searching for an opening. Cool water dripped down Esperanza's face, yet every part of his body seemed to be on fire.

Devona was grinning now. Her eyes were wild, filled with bloodlust. The soaked hair stuck to her face almost made her seem like a madwoman. It appeared that she knew it was only a matter of time before she'd get to finish Esperanza off.

He wasn't going down so easy. Esperanza placed his hand behind his back. Time to protect those broken fingers. He stood slightly sideways, knees bent, weight on the balls of his feet as he took a fencer's stance. His right hand was up. He attacked with a variety of short, quick kicks; kept moving in and out, in and out. Devona managed to cut him a couple of times, but nothing serious. He crouched low. She rushed forward, knife stabbing, but he sidestepped just as the blade was about to enter his belly. He caught her wrist and used her forward motion to throw her off balance, pulled her in a circle as he got her in a lock. She managed to stomp him on the shin and broke free as he fell to one knee. Esperanza thought his shin might be shattered. He tried to put weight on it, but couldn't. He wasn't sure if he'd be able to get back on his feet.

Devona stood a couple of feet away. She used her forearm to wipe wet hair and rainwater from her eyes. A flash of lightning glinted dramatically off the knife in her hand. She was breathing heavy. She seemed frustrated, somewhat uncertain as she took deep breaths, and her eyes became unfocused. Thunder roared and it seemed as if the wooden walkway actually shook.

"I ain't got all day, Devona," Esperanza said in a mocking tone.

This made her mad. Her perfectly plucked eyebrows knotted and her intense eyes squinted.

"Why don't you just die already?"

There he was, on one knee, like he was proposing to Devona. Almost made him laugh out loud. "What's the matter, you stupid bitch?" Esperanza needed to make her lose control. "Too scared to try and finish me off? I thought you might have more balls than your punk husband." He smirked. "I never did tell you, he cried out like a helpless little bitch when I jammed my gun to his head."

Devona shrieked. It was a crazy, ear-piercing shriek, filled with unbearable pain and hate. She clutched the knife tightly in her fist, held it high over her head, and then charged forward. She was about to bring the blade down and kill Esperanza when she suddenly froze. Confused eyes went wide. Mouth was slightly open.

She looked down and it took her a moment to realize that Esperanza stabbed her in the stomach.

The switchblade with the pearl handle had been in his back pocket this whole time. Until he thought he might need to use it. She never saw it coming.

"Wait . . . you . . ."

He drew the blade out and she stumbled backward, dropped the combat knife, and clutched her stomach wound. In the darkness and with the rain falling, Esperanza couldn't see the blood oozing from her. But he could smell it.

Devona looked scared. Scared to die.

"I never said I'd play fair," Esperanza said. There was no irony in his tone. It was simple, matter-of-fact. "Now you can join Rybak in hell."

Though it caused agonizing pain, he managed to get to his feet and then limped forward, switchblade in his left hand.

"Prick."

"You should've never come back, Devona."

Esperanza placed his right hand behind her head and plunged the knife one more time.

He stared deep into her eyes, watching as life began to fade. Esperanza leaned forward and kissed her lips. Softly. Ever so softly. Tasted the salty blood in her mouth. Pulled her into a close embrace, his nose nuzzling her neck as he took in her scent for the final time. He found himself overwhelmed with emotion.

Sadness.

Desire.

Relief.

Devona was right, he'd killed a part of himself; but it was okay. It was time for him to be free.

Esperanza lifted his head and stared into her serene eyes as the Reaper's shadow gently fell across her pupils and her pupils became dim, and then, once and for all, Mistress Devona Love was finally dead.

Chapter
30

He'd never had to dispose of a body before. It gave him a strange, queasy sensation in the pit of his stomach and it made him feel like he was a criminal.

But he did what was necessary.

Esperanza drove across town, through rain-soaked streets, finally on his way home. He was dizzy and his vision was blurred and at times he thought he might pass out. Getting rid of a body was hard work. He wrapped Devona's corpse in a tarp, threw her in the trunk of his car, and drove to the 79th Street Boat Basin. Then he took his Sea Ray 52 Sundancer sports yacht out to the middle of the ocean. There'd been plenty of fun parties on the fifty-three-foot yacht, but he never thought it would help him conceal a crime. Esperanza weighed her corpse down with barbells. Took a shower, bandaged himself, and changed. All of it was made much more difficult because of the incessant rain. But rain was good. Rain washed away evidence. By the time he made it back to the marina, Esperanza was exhausted and in excruciating pain. One of the cuts needed stitches and he knew his ribs were broken.

He went to see Dr. Donato, who stitched him up, gave him a shot of morphine, and told him his ribs were fractured and he'd better not move around much. He also said that if Esperanza wasn't such a good friend he would've called the police about the obvious knife wounds and assault. Instead, he gave Esperanza a cherry lollypop and told him to go home and sleep for a couple of days.

Santos was splayed out on the sofa, his Glock resting on his lap, when Esperanza rushed into the living room. Both of Santos's eyes were black and blue and his nose was swollen. The man looked like he'd been put through the wringer and then some. Santos put the Glock on the coffee table and stood up, and when Esperanza gave him a big bear hug, he let out a yelp.

"Easy, big boy."

"Sorry," Esperanza said as he held Santos by the chin and inspected his nose. "I think it's broken."

"The great detective. Lucky that's all that's broken after the beating I took from King Kong."

"You look like shit."

"You don't look much better, my friend."

"Why haven't you gone to the hospital?"

"I didn't want to leave Legs by herself."

"I appreciate that." Esperanza's eyes nervously darted back and forth. "Where is she?"

"Bedroom. Taking a nap."

Esperanza stroked Santos's cheek. "I'll call a car service to take you to the hospital."

"I can drive myself."

"Not a good idea." Esperanza squeezed his ex-partner's shoulders. "You should've called me earlier, Santos. Instead of going out on your own."

"Yeah, I know. But I decided to do things *your* way for once." He tried to slip on his coat and was having some difficulty, so Esperanza lent him a hand. "But never again, I can tell you that."

"What now?"

"What do you mean?"

"Are you going to Captain Killian and have an investigation started?"

Santos frowned as he holstered his 9mm. "No. I don't think you'd get off so easily this time." He picked up his fedora from the sofa and put it on. "I don't know much about what went down and I don't want to know. I was never here. So let's leave it at that."

They shook hands.

"I owe you big time, partner."

Santos managed to smile, said, "That you do," and made a quick exit.

Esperanza dashed off to the bedroom to see Legs.

The reunion between Legs and Esperanza was crazy emotional. Filled with laughter and tears and hugs and kisses, but not a single word, because at that moment, words didn't matter, and in spite of the aches and pains and tiredness and hunger, they ended up making passionate love all over the bedroom.

They were cuddled up in bed now, basking in the afterglow of their lovemaking, wrapped in each other's arms, exhausted bodies barely able to move. The rain finally stopped.

Legs, her head resting on Esperanza's chest, sat up, propped a couple of pillows against the headboard, and made herself comfortable. Esperanza knew this meant she wanted to talk, so he also sat up and said, "What's up, *mami*?"

Her expression was relaxed. She seemed incredibly calm. Almost glowing. "I have to know . . . Devona?"

"Dead."

"You sure?"

"I killed her. Looked into her eyes when she died." He stroked his swollen jaw. It was getting harder to talk. "So yes, I'm sure."

"How did she die?"

"You don't want to know. Certain questions I'm not gonna answer."

"You trying to protect my emotions?"

He wagged his head and took her hand. "No. I know you can handle anything. But serious crimes have been committed. There are a lot of dead bodies. If the cops ever come around asking questions, the less you know, the better."

She nodded, pushed her hair behind her ears. "Did you fuck her?"

"No."

"You can tell me, it's okay. I understand your obsession now. Devona has this incredible power . . ."

Esperanza squeezed her hand. "*Had.*"

Legs carefully climbed on his lap so that they were face-to-face. She rested her arms around his neck, and Esperanza's hands danced along the small of her back and along her wonderful, broad hips. It brought him great joy to be caressing her naked body once again.

"Do you want to know what happened between Devona and me?"

This might open a whole can of worms. He wasn't ready to deal with it and neither was she. "Not right now. At some point we'll talk about all this. But not now." Esperanza pulled her close and gave her a soft kiss and brushed his nose against hers. "I'm just glad you're safe. You're home. That's all that matters to me."

"You think what happened is gonna change a lot of things between us?"

"Maybe. But we'll deal with it as we've dealt with everything else. We'll get through it."

"You're right." Legs smiled brightly and gazed at him, eyes brimming with tenderness. "Thank you for risking so much for me."

Tears welled up in his eyes. She cocked her head to the side and seemed perplexed by his reaction.

He said, "I'd give my life for you, you know."

She grinned this time. Big, fat grin. Such a sense of pure joy. It made him smile and he pulled her close and squeezed her tight. Legs whispered in his ear, "Yeah. I know. You'd do anything for me."

They held each other like that for a very, very long time.

Epilogue

Esperanza parked his car in the underground garage across the street from Dr. Donato's office. He was getting his broken fingers and ribs checked out as well as stitches removed.

Already a month had passed since that insane, violent night. The dead Russians had been all over the news. The Feds said it was a major mob war between rival Red Mafiya factions and they'd conduct a full and thorough investigation.

Esperanza's life was gradually returning to normal. There were no more nightmares starring Devona. No more glancing over his shoulder. No more paranoia.

Unfortunately for Legs, she was in the opposite. As tough as she was, she was still struggling with what went down. It was going to take her a very long time to trust anyone new in her life. After the Sister Terez/Devona deception, how could anyone blame her? She buried herself in her work and continued volunteering at the women's center.

She'll be okay. She's strong. It'll take a while, but in time she'll heal. But she'll never be the same. Just like I'll never be the same. In some ways we understand each other better now than we ever did before. We're closer than ever before.

He shut off the engine and unbuckled his seat belt when the driver's side window suddenly exploded and something massive smashed against his temple. Esperanza saw stars and the next thing he knew, incredibly thick fingers wrapped around his neck and dragged him out of the car.

It was some kind of giant. Havelock seemed small in comparison. Except this guy was a white boy. Blond, broad face with a buzz cut. He glowered at Esperanza with stunning, aqua blue eyes.

He bounced Esperanza against the doors of a parked SUV with such force it left deep dents in the vehicle. *That hurt.*

Everything was happening so fast, the shocks of pain shooting through his body were making Esperanza delirious, and for a moment it was difficult for him to focus on his attacker so he could defend himself.

After getting slammed against the SUV a couple more times, Esperanza found himself on the hood of his own car.

His attacker's face was red with rage and he was choking the life out of Esperanza. He started to become a blur.

This big fucker's gotta be Otto. He came to finish the job for Devona.

Esperanza needed to be careful because of his broken fingers. He jammed his thumbs into Otto's pretty eyes. The giant screamed and stumbled back, the palms of his hands covering his injured eyeballs. He was fortunate Esperanza hadn't managed to gouge them out.

Esperanza slid off the hood of the car, managed to catch his breath and find his bearings.

Though half blinded, Otto took a wild, uncontrolled

swing and put all his weight behind it. Esperanza ducked and delivered a wicked, short right hook to the kidneys.

That slowed down Otto a little, but didn't stop him.

He lunged at Esperanza with open arms and attempted to get him in a bear hug. Esperanza had no intention of getting crushed. He dropped onto his right knee and his right fist shot straight out, smashing into Otto's groin. The giant howled in pain, and as he dropped to his knees Esperanza swung his forearm and rammed it into Otto's nose and shattered bone.

Quickly getting to his feet, Esperanza went to work on Otto and dished out a relentless barrage of ruthless, powerful blows to every part of the big man's body. Esperanza used his forearms, elbows, knees, and feet, his body becoming a deadly weapon, his mind overtaken with bloodlust.

You think you can take me down, motherfucker? You hurt my girl, now you come after me? I'm gonna put you in a fuckin' wheelchair.

By the time Esperanza was done with Otto, the giant was on the ground, hands trying to protect his head as Esperanza viciously kicked him in the ribs a couple more times.

"Please stop," Otto pleaded. He was sobbing. "Please . . ." Otto held his right hand, palm out, fingers spread wide apart, while his left forearm continued to cover his face. It was a sign of surrender.

Esperanza saw his own reflection in the shiny door of a black Nissan. He stood over Otto, panting. There were specks of blood dotting his face and his jacket. His eyes were as cold as any of the dozens of murderers he'd encountered over the years. He wasn't sure what had taken more out of him, getting tossed around by Otto, or giving the big man the beat down of a lifetime.

So this is what you've become. Straight-up killing machine. Still, isn't this what you were trained to be? A living weapon? But where's the detachment? Where's the stoicism? You crossed that line a long time ago, and it makes you no different from the killers who come after you.

"Why?" Otto asked, dropped his forearm and looked up as Esperanza stared back at him. Blood, snot, and tears snaked down his terrified face. His nose was mush; both eyes were practically swollen shut, and his front teeth were missing. It seemed liked somebody had just worked the guy over with a baseball bat.

"Why what?"

"You took Mistress Love away." It was all a bunch of mumbles. It was a ridiculous cliché, but he sounded like a child who desperately wanted his mommy. Esperanza tried to think of something to say. Nothing came to mind. "What am I supposed to do now?" Otto let out a high-pitched wail and his body heaved. The physical pain wasn't causing it. It was purely emotional. "I'm nothing without her." Esperanza didn't know how to respond to that. "I can't live without my Mistress," Otto added.

Otto's sobbing was so loud and out of control it made Esperanza take a step back. Devona had left him broken and so dependent that without her, Otto was only a shell of a man.

His muscles uncoiled and his body relaxed and Esperanza continued to stare at the pathetic heap of human flesh. What should he do with him? Kill him? No, there'd been enough killing. Besides, Otto was no real threat. He obviously wasn't any kind of professional, just one of Devona's devoted and misguided slaves.

Esperanza pulled a bandana from his pocket and wiped the blood from his hand, knuckles, and face. He gave Otto one last look, then sadly shook his head and walked away.

As he marched through the parking lot, he thought about how much Otto needed Devona. How Devona needed Rybak.

How he needed Legs.

Pain and pleasure. Love and hate. Eternal partners in this dance called life.

All Esperanza wanted was to get out of town for a while, spend some time in the sun and surf of Puerto Rico, and help Legs heal.

And hopefully regain a lost part of his soul in the process.